W9-DCH-096

THE ICEMAN
CHECKS OUT

By Linda Morrison Spear

Monsters are real; ghosts are too.
They live inside us and sometimes they win.
Stephen King

<u>Prologue</u>

On the day Robert Bryce Swaine, vice president of Clearview Chemicals corporate departments was found murdered, the mood at the New York site of his corporation went from its normal shade of gloom to positively jubilant. Yes, even though the specter of murder gave his worker bees a shudder or two, life suddenly had suddenly become a whole lot sweeter.

Swaine had been found slumped over his desk, surrounded by a foot-high stack of file folders, one arm rigidly extended. His assistant, Miriam, had actually thought he was catnapping when she finally overcame her hesitation and entered his office. He would usually yell "NOT NOW!" in response to her persistent knocks, which she was forced to do when he closeted himself away despite the relentlessly ringing phones clamoring for his attention.

But Swaine didn't like others to make decisions without his approval, and on this particular morning, everything was stalled by his silence, upping the already high stress level among his staff.

"Mr. Swaine," Miriam called out in her most soothing voice as she pressed the door open a crack. "Mr. Swaine," she said again, almost apologetically. "I'm sorry, but I really must have a moment of your time."

When no reply came, she reluctantly opened the door all the way and tiptoed toward the slumped figure on his desk. How odd, she thought. He must have fallen asleep. Do I dare try to wake him up, or am I asking for immediate termination?

And then she noticed the large pool of blood neatly framing his head. She threw her head back, emitted a blood-curdling scream, and ran out of the office yelling, "Call 911!"

Linda Spear

Chapter One

Thursday, January 2

The long clumping strides, combined with the sound of squirting fluid and crunching ice that sprang from R.B. Swaine's boots, alerted those who had already arrived at Clearview Chemicals to his entry into the Corporate Relations Department on that cold, snowy day.

The sounds were made by feet that were well more than a full foot in length and attached to a drenched, brown-clothed tree trunk of a man.

Swaine walked down the carpeted passageway toward the end of the hall, his coat and boots left pellets of ice along the way. As he continued on his way through the department, he peered into the offices of those who would directly report to him. A derisive smile creased his face as he took note if they were the early ones or the late comers.

With pock-marked features, evidence of an acne-ravaged adolescence, and a head considerably out of proportion to his body, nothing was likely to interfere with this man on a mission.

Swaine stomped doggedly forward, aiming for the corner office to the left with floor-to-ceiling windows.

He had recently gained a venerable position in the corporate departments as the newly appointed Vice President of Administration, and on that day he decided to make a highly visible entrance to his stylish quarters at Clearview Chemicals.

Moments after the elongated body of the man propelled itself past Lydia Barrett's office door, she heard a voice, which sounded less than human and more like a moose in heat, call out, "Hey, where's the goddamned light switch in this place?"

Lydia, Manager of External Communications at the chemical

company, rose quickly from her desk chair, leaving behind a sheaf of papers and a partially eaten glazed donut with a steaming cup of coffee, to look down the hallway in the direction of the voice.

Swaine's large shadow hung in the doorway molding of his new office as he rejected the notion of entering the darkened interior without the assistance of overhead light. His hand futilely groped the wall surrounding the doorjamb for the switch. He muttered impatiently as he waited for the help he had summoned to arrive.

Lydia watched anxiously as her own secretary, Angela Guttierez, dashed down the hall to the office, brushed by the man in the doorway, and quickly located the switch on the wall.

"Who the hell decided to put the light switch there," he bellowed to the assistant, who had succeeded where he failed.

"I don't know, sir. I'll try to find out."

"Why?" he growled. "It was only a rhetorical question." He replied with obvious disdain and looked down at Angela to say, "But you wouldn't know what rhetorical means, would you, Chiquita." He laughed derisively and turned his back on the surprised woman.

"I know what rhetorical means," she mumbled to herself in outrage.

Lydia watched sympathetically as Angela ran quickly back by her own office and shot a disparaging look in the direction of Swaine. Impulsively, Lydia pursued her down the hallway into the women's restroom, located around the corner. There she found the secretary dabbing her eyes with tissue in a vain attempt not to disturb her makeup.

"Aw, Angie. I'm so sorry you had to start off with that guy in such a crappy way."

Lydia, clearly concerned for her administrative assistant, placed her hand gently on the girl's shoulder.

Blackened tears began to stream onto Angie's clean white sweater and were doomed to remain there all day long.

"That asshole tried to make a fool out of me, just for helping him find his light switch," she said, angrily attempting to stem the tears that continued to pour from her eyes.

"He just felt stupid for not being able to find the switch himself," Lydia said sympathetically, and added, "but that doesn't excuse his behavior."

"Well, he'd better cut that crap out. He called me 'Chiquita,' that racist bastard," replied Angie as she turned to face Lydia. With more control she added, "But I know what you mean. I'll get it together, wash the eye makeup off my new sweater and steer clear of him. You know, my mother gave this cashmere beauty to me for Christmas. I can't believe it's ruined already. But thanks for your support, Lydia. That Swaine freak really is an insensitive jerk."

As Angela soaked up a paper towel with soap and water to attack the stains on her sweater, she brightened, somewhat, and said, "Happy New Year, Lydia. What a hell of a way to welcome it in at work." Lydia nodded in agreement.

The two women worked together to wash the makeup off the sweater and only succeeded in leaving small gray smudges and the knowledge that a trip to the local dry cleaners would be necessary.

As they walked slowly back to the department, Angela continued the few steps further down the hallway to her cubicle, located diagonally across from Swaine's now brightly lit office. By the time Lydia returned to her desk, a growing sense of apprehension enveloped her. In the short time since she had passed through the security station, situated at the main entrance of the compound early that morning, Lydia knew this was going to be a difficult beginning to the new year. She now realized that the damaging stories she had heard about R.B. Swaine's prior behavior, before his arrival at Clearview, were evidently true.

Carrying her unfinished donut and the remainder of her coffee, she crossed the hallway and entered the office of Christina Benderhoff. Christina and Lydia, both single women in their mid-thirties, had shared a comfortable friendship from the first day that Christina arrived on site two years earlier.

Without ceremony, Lydia sank into one of the chairs that faced her colleague's desk. Christina, a specialist attached to the internal communications section of the Corporate Relations Department, was the person with whom Lydia was most relaxed at the office. She also felt at ease entering the office unannounced at this time of the day because she knew her friend would most likely be feasting on her daily breakfast of a cranberry-orange muffin, vitamin pills, and decaf tea.

Christina was the prototypical creature of habit. At eight in the morning, when she arrived at work to perform her job as the writer of the company's internal promotional materials and speeches, she sat at her impeccably neat desk, checked her voicemail to see if anyone had left a message for her after she had left the office the night before. There was rarely a message to return because Christina usually left late in the evening. She, in fact, was renowned for the number of hours she worked in the day.

Her ex-husband had once remarked during their brief marriage that if she came home any later, she would have to start back to the site before she arrived at the front door of their house.

Not one to actively complain about job stress, or the disaster that had been her recently dissolved marriage, Christina exhibited sensory overload, with eyes that wore the weariness of heavy lids with puffy baggage. It was hard to know if Christina's look of exhaustion was the result of genetics or was brought on by what she acknowledged to have been a "bitch of a year."

After searching for the usually non-existent phone messages at the beginning of each workday, Christina, without fail, unpacked a brown paper bag from her simple canvas World Wildlife Fund carryall. She removed several paper napkins from the top of the bag, spreading them down on her desk as a placemat for her coffee and muffin, which she carefully positioned side by side.

Christina was between bites of her muffin when Lydia arrived at her door. Brightened by the sight of her colleague, she motioned for Lydia to sit down.

"Did you hear the first fireworks of the day?" Lydia asked her friend.

"What do you mean?" mumbled Christina, looking up, mouth full, as she continued to eat her muffin.

"Swaine does not tread lightly on this planet," Lydia replied, and she related the incident with Angela.

"How could he tread lightly with those feet?" Christina chuckled, and took a sip of her tea. "I watched him pass by here on his way down the hall. Did you hear those squishing sounds coming from his shoes? He sounded like a large animal on the prowl, not that I've seen many large animals in heat." Christina burst out laughing. Lydia remained unamused.

"No, I'm serious, Chris. If this is the kind of treatment we can expect from this guy, we're in for a tough time. And that new assistant of his that he brought along, Ms. Ass-Kiss, or whatever her name is, does not return phone calls or respond to memos that are issued to confirm any appointments.

"I'd say she's in her early fifties or so, and has the most vacant face I've ever seen," added Lydia. "She can't seem to pull it all together. I heard she was known to organize meetings for Swaine at his last job that involved company representatives who had to fly to corporate headquarters where they worked before. She could have easily arranged for phone or Skype meetings. Twice, I heard from people I know, she simply forgot to inform several company representatives that the meetings had been canceled, and the representatives appeared on time for a non-existent gathering."

Christina practically coughed up her muffin at the thought. "Swaine either doesn't know or overlooks these issues, but he's apparently entranced by her breathy voice and the way she answers the phone. I think she could make a decent living in iPad porn."

Christina finished her cup of tea and added, "When she speaks, she sounds as if she's about to start a eulogy. But if it was for Swaine, there would be a lot of empty seats in the funeral parlor."

Lydia laughed heartily at her friend's assessment of the two new residents of the department.

"I hate to bring it up again," Christina said cautiously, "because I know how you feel about bigots, but do you think he treated Angela so badly because she's a Latina, or is it just that she's an administrative assistant and he thinks he can treat support staff that way?"

Lydia balled up the napkin she used to wipe the donut crumbs from her face and fired it, plus her empty coffee cup, at the wastebasket five feet away and said, "I don't know, but if that's the case, it's even worse than I thought."

Chapter Two

Cal Ferguson always considered himself to be the most careful man on site. His job as the Director of Health, Safety, and Environmental Compliance charged him with the responsibility of ensuring the safety of the 2,175 people who arrived at the company each day to earn a living. Ferguson, secure in his ability to do the job, recognized that a site of almost seventy acres and ten buildings could create challenges that could cause the work done in the chemical research labs and administrative office facilities to periodically conflict.

Ferguson's hard-hat mentality was often the butt of jokes on days when the buildings were periodically evacuated due to laboratory accidents that produced chemical odors throughout the connecting buildings. His short, stout body and carefully combed over blond hair could always be seen, bobbing up between layers of employees who lined the perimeter of the site. Until Ferguson himself declared the "all clear" signal through his beloved bullhorn, no one reentered the buildings.

Everyone who knew Ferguson accepted the fact that he savored the power of his position. He was known, at the times of building evacuation, for saying to those in the crowd, "I'm in charge here," in the event that people did not recognize his role.

Ferguson also held the responsibility for recognizing and eliminating safety infractions found in the offices of those of varying degrees of importance. It was not beyond him to tell a vice president to rearrange furniture found in that office so that wiring was not exposed to walking areas within the office. Yet no one believed for one second that Ferguson understood the elements of Feng Shui. No doubt, he believed that it was definitely Asian and obviously edible.

The story that followed the mere mention of his name raised him to almost legendary status. One morning, Ferguson walked into the office of a high-ranking senior manager and demanded that he rid the office of overflowing mounds of paper that threaded up the walls toward the ceiling and over every square inch of floor. When the executive told him to get out, Ferguson succinctly said to the man that the mess presented a fire hazard, and advised him to remove the debris within forty-eight hours or Cal would be forced to condemn the office until the work could be done to his satisfaction. The executive, people were told, simply closed his eyes, shook his head, smirked, and went back to work.

Two mornings later, when the executive arrived for work, he found his office door closed and the lock changed. A large "condemned" sign was stuck to the center of the door.

Ferguson casually loped down the hall and arrived at the executive's office some few minutes later. He advised the enraged man that his phone had been forwarded to the vacant desk near his office, and that he could work at that station until his office had been cleared. The key to the furious executive's office could be found in his superior's office, and was to be used and then be returned at the end of each cleaning session, until the office could again be considered safe for occupancy.

The executive, as the story goes, went directly to the Chief Executive Officer, Charles Wainwright, declared his outrage, and demanded that Cal Ferguson be fired on the spot. But Wainwright had been advised of the situation by Ferguson days before, and staunchly stood by his safety inspector.

The executive cursed under his breath all the way back to his office and demanded the help of all the secretaries within the department.

When the office was neat and spotless by noon of the very same day, he hastily sat down at his clean desk and slammed the door shut, never to be seen again until he was ready to depart for the evening.

Despite the fact that Ferguson was viewed as a crusading clown, he was silently respected for his actions by those who could be saved at a time of trouble on site.

Chapter Three

Lydia Barrett caught a glimpse of Ferguson as he meandered through the linking corridors. As he passed Lydia's door, he was tempted to stop even before she called him because it was well known that her office was always the source of gooey sweet comfort food just at the time when one could use it most.

"Hey, Cal," Lydia called to him as he stopped at her doorway. "Want to share a package of TastyKake Butterscotch Krimpets with me? I can assure you the offer holds for only thirty seconds."

Cal always wondered how anyone could eat as much as Lydia and not get fat. It'll catch up with her someday, he figured, but for now he'd put that thought aside and enter her office to help her polish off the delicacy that she so generously offered.

"I love this stuff. Where do you get these things?" he asked her as he plunged himself into the nearest seat and took a Krimpet from the package. "I never can find them at the supermarkets around here."

"Actually, I get my stash from a secret supplier," she replied coyly. "You know I grew up outside of Philly, and butterscotch Krimpets were staples to my diet and almost everyone else who I knew there. When I came to live in New York, I couldn't find them in any store and found out they aren't distributed all over the country. So, I had to take matters into my own hands."

She leaned back in her desk chair, placed her feet on the top of her wastebasket, and licked each finger that was covered with frosting appreciatively. Cal tried to ignore the suggestive moves she made, as he didn't want Lydia to know how attracted to her he had become.

"I persuaded my sister, who still lives in the old hometown, to send me a case every month. It's no big deal for her to go to the local supermarket,

Linda Spear

buy them for me, then take the stash to the post office for mailing. In exchange, I FedEx a dozen freshly baked New York bagels to her every Friday morning."

"You always find a way to get what you want, don't you?" said Ferguson appreciatively, as he sank his teeth into his first bite of Krimpet.

"What's that supposed to mean, Cal?" asked Lydia, who stiffened slightly and looked quizzically at the man.

"It's no secret, Lydia, that when you speak up around here, you get heard." He watched her face change as he stated the facts, and added, "That's not to say that you get away with anything you shouldn't. God knows, everyone around here respects you and admires the way you manage people. It's just that you're so…outspoken, and no one ever seems to smack you down."

Lydia relaxed slightly, took another bite of her Krimpet, and said, "I don't get away with anything, Cal. That's just crap. I say what's on my mind, and when it makes sense to the head honchos, and it's right for Clearview Chemicals, I don't get punished for saying what needs to be said."

She polished off the Krimpet and added, "I think I'll have to reconsider my communication techniques somewhat from now on. Did you see what just blew in from the cold this morning?"

"Are you referring to R.B. Swaine?" asked Ferguson. "Actually, yes, I'm referring to the Really Big Swine, Cal. You should have seen how that jerk made his entrance this morning. It's as though he had successfully completed a bloodless coup on a vulnerable country and made himself at home in the newly occupied territory."

"Have you seen Macomber since he arrived?" Ferguson referred to Lydia's boss, the Director of Corporate Relations, Daniel J. Macomber.

"No, I expect he'll be calling me and the other managers into his office very soon, though," she said, tossing her napkin into the wastebasket. "I can wait."

Ferguson checked his tie and dusted his clothing after finishing his TastyKake treat.

"Never know whether the wrapping paper from the TastyKakes should go in the recycling bin," he muttered to himself, "because they are not technically considered clean refuse…oh well. Anyway, I'm on my way to Frenkle's office. He's sweating bricks over Swaine's arrival."

Ferguson paused for a moment, deciding whether to reveal the rest of what he planned to say then continued. "You know full well that we've had a rash of reports of suspected environmentally induced illnesses in some of our buildings. Swaine will be out to axe all of our heads if he can find a scapegoat, especially if the media finds out. Frenkle and I don't want to be on his hit parade."

Lydia nodded as she acknowledged what Cal said. She had, indeed, heard reports of suspected illnesses that suggested a chemical or chemicals may be contaminating certain buildings on site, and she was concerned about her required response should word get out to the press.

Although she had not suffered any symptoms, she had documented the concerns of several people from her own staff on medical data forms and sent them to Paul Frenkle's office.

"What do you think is causing it, Cal? Do we really have sick buildings or do we just have a virus floating through the site that causes the illnesses?"

Cal stood up, shook each leg to straighten his trouser pants, and said, "I really don't know for sure at this point, Lydia. I'd like to believe that it's something simple like a crappy little winter bug that's highly contagious and has nothing to do with the buildings, but I'm not putting any money on a theory yet. I will keep you informed, though."

As he turned to leave, he looked at Lydia still cleaning her desk of Krimpet debris and said appreciatively, "I don't know how you stay looking so good with what you pack it away, lady, but I'd love to know your secret."

Lydia chuckled and replied, "I guess it's because of my job. You know, all that running in place, chasing my ass…"

Cal laughed out loud as he waved goodbye and rounded the corner of the corridor in a forward trajectory to see his boss, Site Director Paul Frenkle.

Chapter Four

Frenkle nervously sifted through the ever-increasing stack of forms, which detailed reports of employee illness or injury on the job, such as headaches, nausea, dizziness and the like. Although it was only 9:30 in the morning, his rumpled brown suit looked as though he had come to work having slept in it. He was the consummate company man, but without question he already despised Swaine. The newly emerged head of the corporate departments had already spent unlimited hours going through Frenkle's people, his departments, and his operation with an eye toward disassembly long before Swaine even arrived on site.

Frenkle was not known to be a trendsetter, but he was well respected for his straightforward method of handling tricky situations that routinely popped up on site. He was first to remind himself that to work for a chemical company in an increasingly environmentally-conscious society was to constantly be on guard against shooting oneself in the foot.

"I'm doing the best that I can," he thought to himself as he recalled how he had spent what was meant to be family time during the holiday season entrenched in the paperwork that showed every indication of the troubling air quality within the buildings. All the while, he dreamed of the coming baseball season.

Whenever noxious chemical odors inadvertently leaked from the research labs or beyond, a significant number of employees became ill in Office Buildings One and Two. How fumes from the lab and science buildings could cause illness in adjacent areas that were not directly connected greatly disturbed him.

What also irked him was that Swaine could become privy to this information and turn it against him for not solving the problem before his arrival.

Frenkle hunched over the mounting reports of "foul air related illness" in Office Building Two and shook his head. His body jerked stiffly to attention as he heard a knock on his door.

Cal Ferguson entered Frenkle's office, an iPhone securely planted in his closed fist, and made sure to close the door firmly behind him. Ferguson tried to make this gesture seem natural when sensitive matters were to be discussed.

In the ten years that Frenkle had been Site Director, Ferguson had been part of his staff in various capacities for the majority of the time.

"What the hell is going on in these buildings?" he hissed at Ferguson who had not yet reached a chair to sit down. Ferguson was unsure as to whether he should sit or remain standing in place as he thought about what to say.

"It's hard to figure what is causing the presumed illnesses, sir. There's even the possibility, although I hope not, that some people are using our investigation of potential toxicity to take sick days." Ferguson was surprised to see Frenkle look at him in disbelief.

"You can't be serious," he shouted. Realizing that his angry response could potentially be heard by the assistants on the other side of the door, he automatically lowered his voice and said, "That's bullshit, and you know it. No one needs to cook up illness and blame it on a sick building to take off a few days of work at this company. That's why we have an unlimited sick day policy. You know full well that a number of studies conducted by human resource consultants all over this country attest to the fact that when employees are not restricted to a specific number of sick days a year, they tend to take less time off than people who work at companies that have a defined limit.

"These reports that I have here are from the employees' doctors who are concerned about the symptoms and have asked us to investigate the possibility of varying levels of toxicity in the buildings. That's not just employees having a case of the 'vapors,' Ferguson!"

Cal looked sheepish as he said, "I just thought we should consider it as an unlikely alternative, sir. It seems to me that sometimes the things that seem so complex have simple answers if only we are open to them." Ferguson shifted his ample weight from foot to foot and backed up slightly toward the door.

"Well, damned if I know what the answer is, but you better get your ass in gear and find out real quick, or we'll both be out on permanent unpaid sick leave."

Chapter Five

By the time Daniel J. Macomber decided to call his managers into his office for a confidential meeting at nine in the morning on the first day following the New Year break, he had chewed through six coffee stirrer straws.

Macomber had quit smoking two weeks before Christmas and found that he could subdue his enormous oral fixation, somewhat, by chewing plastic straws. He kept a small supply in the upper right-hand drawer of his desk, where he used to keep his ever-present box of Macanudo cigars.

Macomber, a man of respectability and a heavy dose of propriety, had the good sense to shut his office door when he felt the need to chew. He knew that his image would suffer if he were noticed with a straw protruding from his teeth as he talked on the phone or conversed with his colleagues.

A cigar, he thought sourly to himself, would certainly appear more acceptable in these circles, but Macomber had less and less options from which to choose these days. He reluctantly gave up his tobacco habit in deference to Fiona, his wife of thirty-four years, who had been recently diagnosed with secondary smoke emphysema.

Considerable guilt, and a hacking smoker's cough of his own, encouraged Daniel J. Macomber to give his last few boxes of Macanudos to an appreciative neighbor.

Macomber was coughing ferociously when Angela Guttierez led the small group of managers into his spacious office. Lydia, as well as Issues Management Chief Randall Goddard, Internal Communications Manager Karen Paulson, Corporate Lobbyist Dean Handlesman, and Art Director Gunnar Williamsen each carried with them a leather folder that held a legal pad, pen, and space for business cards.

"That cough will die down pretty soon, Dan," reassured Randy

Goddard. A reformed ex-smoker, Randy Goddard frequently assumed the role of self-help director for newly smoke-free colleagues whenever he felt needed. "Give it two to three weeks tops, and you'll forget you ever smoked at all."

"I don't give a crap about the cough. It's the stress," barked Macomber as he swung out from behind his desk and headed for the round table at the back of his office where the others had already gathered.

"Sorry for jumping on you, Randy, I'm just mad as hell that I had to give them up just when I need the goddamned things the most."

Lydia and the other members of the small group remained silent, all knowing to which stress he referred. They were also quite surprised at Macomber's unaccustomed public use of foul language and explosion of temper.

Dan Macomber, a thirty-year veteran of the corporation, was a man currently caught in the crossfire. As a newly appointed vice president, Macomber had just begun to enjoy the fruits of his unwavering loyalty to Clearview Chemicals. First, as a manager, then years later as a director, Dan Macomber longed publically and privately for the dignity of the job that eluded him for years. It was finally his. Why wasn't he happy?

Swaine.

"Just a while longer before we can promote you further," Charles B. Wainwright would gently remind him with each yearly review of his accomplishments. There was always just one piece of the puzzle missing.

"Get this one area in shape, and we can get the ball rolling for your promotion."

The promotion to vice president was finally awarded to him with much pomp and circumstance less than two years earlier.

Macomber's plans for a comfortable retirement were now

jeopardized by the arrival of R.B. Swaine. Macomber found his daydreams of the sizeable pension bestowed upon those who are elevated to his current position interrupted by thoughts of potential interference. If the rumors were true, that Swaine had been brought in to flatten the verticality of the corporate departments by weeding out unnecessary levels of management, Macomber's slow departure into a retirement date of his choice could be considerably hastened and decided for him.

Although Macomber knew he had served the company well in the preceding quarter century plus, he was not immune to worry over how relevant his position was perceived by the highest level of management and how important the people in his department were to the workings of the corporation.

Division presidents, he recalled, routinely commented on the fact that they made the various products and earned the money for the corporation, and corporate services simply spent money in their effort to supply services of varying need and importance. How relevant did his operation appear to the division presidents? Did they talk about him behind his back? Was his department in danger of being carved up among the divisions, and would a portion of his staff be laid off?

Macomber had a lot more on his mind these days than how much better his smoker's cough would be in a few weeks.

Chapter Six

"You're probably wondering why I called this last-minute meeting on the first day back after the holidays. I'm sure you figured it had to do with next week's Communicator's Conference," he began. Suddenly pausing, he said, "Nah, why bother with the crapola. You all know why you're here." He leaned back in his chair, glanced up at the ceiling, and looked back at his desk. All those seated at the table knew he could have used a straw to chew on.

"R.B. Swaine, who I will from now on refer to as 'The Pontiff,' is not just the head of our department. In fact," Macomber said disconsolately, "he is the life and death of all the corporate departments, and he wants to hold a full group meeting with our unit at eleven o'clock sharp this morning in the conference room. Be there on time. In fact, be fifteen minutes early."

Still, no one responded to his words, and they waited for him to say more. R.B. Swaine, everyone now knew, was now the chief of all the other corporate departments throughout the States.

"I invited you in here to give you some background on Swaine. I think it's important that you prepare your people, before the meeting, to expect some changes in the way we run things in our department. You can explain this best by calling your own section members into your offices as soon as we break from this meeting."

Karen Paulson, manager of the internal communications section, spoke first.

"Dan, does this mean that we will be required to alter our basic routine in any significant way?" She asked this question as much with her hands as her voice. Karen, an expensively dressed woman with an edge, was in her late-thirties. She was forceful in her manner and used both hands to emphasize whatever point she made. Her vigorous gestures assured her of a rapt audience.

Linda Spear

The narrow frame set on a diminutive body belied the resilient fiber from which Karen Paulson was crafted. As she looked directly at her boss, there was no doubt that her concerns were focused solely on her own performance standards.

"To be perfectly frank, Karen, I don't think he'll be looking to change the way you do things," he said with a half-smile fighting its way to his face.

She looked surprised as Macomber made the unsubtle reference to her style of management, and, at first, attempted to ignore the sarcasm attached to his remark.

Karen managed instead to temper her apparent indignation and coyly replied, "Does that mean Swaine likes high-octane executives, Dan?"

Goddard, a portly man, uncomfortably seated in a tight chair, stared down at his hands that rested on his paunch. Lydia doodled idly on her writing tablet as impeccably dressed and groomed Handlesman, seated beside her, placed his hands on the back of his head, stretched his arms, and looked toward the ceiling in a posture he recalled his father taking whenever Handlesman's outspoken Italian mother had something irrelevant to say.

Handlesman was known to be indispensable to Clearview Chemicals. Tall, dark haired, and intense in his approach, he was proud of his Italian heritage and the determination of his German father's ancestry. He knew how to approach every congressman or legislator and remembered personal facts about each of them in order to ingratiate himself to the people who proposed bills that could alter the future of the company.

Only tall, blond, and sophisticated Swedish-born Williamsen, dressed in casual slacks and an open-collared shirt, continued to listen impassively. Gunnar Williamsen had been in the United States for less than two years, and was uncertain as to what was appropriate to say and do at a time like this.

Macomber reached across the table and covered Karen's hand with his own.

"That means, my dear, that his style is touted to be similar to your own, and you may be the only one among us who will, in his estimation, measure up to his requirements."

Karen smiled slightly as she pulled her hand from under his and relaxed again in her chair. She, after all, needed few reminders that she was a woman of tremendous ambition, driven to achievement that far exceeded the specifications of her job.

Karen was also quite satisfied that she was admired at a distance by most men at Clearview Chemicals for her well-kept figure, subtly highlighted shoulder-length hair, and expertly made-up face.

The distance and aloof stance she maintained, however, was believed to have been carefully developed and practiced over the years to let few people know much more about her than her job title. Her private life, she reminded herself repeatedly, was not for public domain. Her staff, to which Christina Benderhoff belonged, knew precious little about the woman with whom they worked, except for the fact that she had been married once, that her family consisted only of her widowed father who lived hundreds of miles away in Ohio, and her cat, Domino, to whom she awarded singular devotion.

Karen thought of her cat, as she often did in tense situations, as Macomber continued his conversation with his managers.

"What I'm saying is that Swaine has what we could call 'an aggressive style.' I've heard from people who have known him throughout the industry that he comes into every arena with a preconceived strategic plan.

"He's a product of an Ivy League education and a privileged upbringing, and he's got a lot of polish when it counts. What you should also know is that he's great at telling those people in charge what they want to hear, and they somehow end up believing what they are told is their own idea.

Linda Spear

"I think Wainwright has already been baffled by Swaine's bullshit. He's placed a lot of faith in that man. As far as what I know of the people Swaine has managed in the past—those who march to his drum, do well, and those who don't… Well, shall we just say they either decide to do it his way or they do it elsewhere."

Handlesman spoke up for the first time. "You sound as if all of our very jobs may be on the line with this guy. Is that what you're saying?"

Macomber switched his chair in another direction and said, "Dean, I'd like to tell you otherwise, but I'm not encouraged by his presence here at Clearview."

Lydia jerked herself forward and angrily retorted, "I can't believe you're already planning to knuckle under to this type of intimidation. You don't really expect us to be totally submissive to poor management, do you?"

When Macomber turned to reply, Lydia was taken aback by the anger in his face.

"Listen, Lydia, I know you like to call a spade a spade, but you better learn to be less direct on this one and keep that kind of comment confined to this group, or even better, to yourself. You could jeopardize more than your own hide if you're not more careful with what you say. We can only hope that Swaine's star, which has risen so fast, will fade in due time."

Macomber rose to end the meeting and pointedly announced to his staff: "One day he's going to get caught up in his own web of deceit."

Lydia's heart raced at the force of the unexpected rage she saw in this decent man's face and began to worry further about her own place in this corporate community.

"And remember, all of you, get yourselves and your people to that meeting on time—no stragglers," Macomber said as he rose from his seat at the round table, returned to the desk at the other end of the room, and reached into his drawer for a straw. He no longer seemed to care who noticed.

Chapter Seven

Clearview Chemicals commenced operations in the late 1950's as a fledgling insecticide manufacturer. The company was so named because of the lush topography that dominated the landscape on which the corporate headquarters of the company was located in upstate New York.

Over the course of fifty-plus years, Clearview had succeeded in creating and subsequently dominating the field of agrochemicals developed to appeal to and supply a continually growing population of environmentally conscious consumers.

"Clearview Chemicals are Green Chemicals," the ads proclaimed. "Clearview has reached the Summit of Safety," others declared. And the Environmental Protection Agency tests proved them right. Clearview was renowned for its safety track record. The corporate headquarters, seat of all new product development, had won the OSHA Star of Distinction award two years in a row—a feat practically unheard of in the chemical industry.

Most proud of this record was Charles B. Wainwright, Chief Executive Officer of the corporation. Wainwright, an attorney by training, had assumed the helm of the company some five years before.

Wainwright had spent his formative years with the company as a legal monitor of the incidents, otherwise known as minor chemical spills, exhaust escapes, and the like, that if known to the public would have proved damaging to the company's image.

Hardcopy documents of these incidents, always referred to as "occurrences," were not kept in the common legal files. They were, instead, originally filed as microfilm, later transferred onto computer flash drives, and locked in Wainwright's office vault for safe keeping.

If "occurrences" happened, or the company became responsible for poor operational planning, Wainwright liked to assure himself that his own environment was kept neat with less chance of unpleasant repercussions.

The Clearview Chemicals Executive Suite was comprised of a two-story modern building attached by a glass enclosed bridge to Office Building One. Modern art and manicured plants adorned the somewhat sterile corridors that intertwined the lavish offices of Clearview Chemicals management, those top executives who strategized and facilitated the growth of the diversified international corporation.

Wainwright sat ensconced in a large corner suite of rooms, which naturally faced the most attractively landscaped area of the seventy acres on the site. Wainwright was highly regarded by his peers in the industry as a brilliant theorist. Those who worked with him were well aware of his vast accomplishments.

In the five years since his appointment to the position of Chief Executive Officer, he had effectively increased the holdings and profits of the diversified company and strategically divested loss leaders acquired under the leadership of the past CEO, long since relegated to retirement.

At age fifty-nine, Wainwright looked a full decade younger than his years. He possessed graying brown hair and stood a shade over six feet in height, with an erect carriage maintained on a spare body. His coterie of vice presidents, many of them years younger, marveled at Wainwright's thick head of barely graying dark brown hair and horned-rim glasses that skillfully shrouded the few wrinkles that had formed around his eyes. Wainwright projected vitality as he guided his management committee through a challenging economic era.

On the morning following the New Year's holiday, Wainwright awaited the arrival of recently hired Vice President R.B. Swaine. The bulging dossier on Swaine was carefully compiled by independent management consultants long before the man was hired. It indicated that Swaine was highly capable of tightening up systems, weeding out unnecessary operations, and creating an atmosphere of discomfort in order to heighten productivity based on a most human fear—job loss.

The profile also stressed the fact that at the height of six foot eight, R.B.'s appearance required people to raise their heads with an appearance of deference to the man.

Swaine's bulbous, heavily veined nose and gangly body frequently produced an adverse response among employees. Unpleasant to look at, unwieldy in his stride, and unwelcome in all of his prior work environments, R.B. Swaine was frequently known in tight circles as "Really Big Swine." Wainwright chuckled as he read about the moniker.

Swaine, he learned, had been so successful in fulfilling his responsibilities at his last position that the employees who remained following the blood bath threw themselves a going away party, in his honor, after he took leave of the company.

Yes, thought Wainwright, the job he had in mind, was well suited to R.B. Swaine. It was not intended for a gentleman. Newly appointed Vice President R.B. Swaine, he recognized, could be quite useful.

A peculiar squishing sound drew Wainwright's attention to the entrance of his office. Without the expected knock on the door to herald a visitor, Wainwright looked up from the dossier to note that the entire door frame was taken up by the length and breadth of R.B. Swaine.

Behind Swaine was Wainwright's assistant, Kay McIntosh, who looked at her employer with anxiety and confusion.

"Mr. Swaine is here to see you, sir," she blurted out almost as an afterthought. "I asked him to wait for me to announce him, but…"

Swaine strode forward and attached his hand to Wainwright's own.

"Glad to be here, Charles," he said. As he picked up a framed portrait from Wainwright's desk, he chuckled appreciatively and said, "Your daughter or a significant other?"

Wainwright had never believed in love at first sight, or hate, for that matter, but his mind was quickly changing.

As Wainwright watched the gangling man in amazement, Swaine responded appreciatively to his own remarks with a peculiar guffaw that sounded to Wainwright like television cartoon character Bullwinkle the Moose addressing Rocky the Squirrel.

"Have a seat, R.B.," Wainwright said, knowing full well he need not offer the amenity; it would be taken, regardless.

Swaine, instead, hands folded behind his back, paced Wainwright's office, surveying mementos displayed on the credenza behind Wainwright's large desk and examining the artwork hung on two walls.

"You like modern?" he asked Wainwright as he leaned closer to one particular painting in what appeared to be his effort to analyze the brush strokes.

"I like a lot of things. Have a seat, R.B."

This time, Swaine complied. Wainwright recalled the commentary found within the confidential report about one of the corporate relations employees at Andrus Chemicals who Swaine decided to eliminate. Wainwright carefully placed the inflammatory file in his desk drawer, and he began to wonder if, perhaps, for the first time in his lengthy professional career, he had made a huge mistake.

*

The Corporate Relations Department Conference Room was filled to overflowing as the full complement of department employees arrived long before the 11:00 am meeting was scheduled to begin.

Although attendance was required at staff meetings, there were never enough chairs to accommodate those who arrived shortly before the meeting commenced. The appropriate number of chairs was never ordered for the room. Staff members were convinced that Macomber wanted to make the subtle point that those who arrived on time got seats and those who did not stood.

What was most unusual about the gathering on this day following New Year's was the sobriety of the attendees.

In the past, small talk accompanied by raucous laughter was common before meetings were officially called to order. What now took its place was sotto-voce murmuring within small clusters as people sat together in familiar and trusted alliances within the group.

As the beeper of Randall Goddard's iPhone alerted everyone that the hour of eleven had arrived and passed without the appearance of the person who called the meeting, Macomber could no longer contain his agitation and said, "Did anyone see 'Ichabod Swaine' before they came in here?" The room remained silent, although almost everyone stifled a laugh.

Seconds passed and Miriam Ashworth volunteered, "He planned to meet with Mr. Wainwright from 9:30 until 10, so I expect that he is still there."

Macomber pushed himself away from the table, strode over to the phone attached to the far wall of the conference room, and thrust it in the direction of Ms. Ashworth.

"Get on the horn and call Wainwright's office. See if Swaine's still there, and tell him we're waiting."

Miriam jumped up from her seat and took the phone from Macomber's hand as if it were a hot potato. As she started punching in numbers, Macomber added, "And while you're at it, get some more goddamned seats for the people without chairs. Why should they have to stand and wait for this guy?"

Ms. Ashworth waited for an answer from Wainwright's office as Macomber paced around the crowded conference room.

Lydia, who was seated between Christina and Dean, turned from one to the other in an effort to assess their thoughts. Christina was threading her hands through her short blond hair—a habit long accepted by her colleagues as evidence of chronic tension. First she raked both sides at the same time with fingers spread to keep the hairstyle uniform, then the left hand swept through the front, pushing it back to balance with the sides. Dean, on the other hand, was rotating his pen between his fingers and appeared to accidently let it slip onto Lydia's lap.

"Are you trying to give me something to do while we wait," she whispered in his ear.

Dean, half smiling, turned partially in her direction and replied, "I didn't intend to, but if you want something to do…"

She giggled quietly as she placed his pen on the empty pad of paper before him on the table.

"You don't trust my aim anymore, do you?"

"Sure I do, Dean," she said chidingly. "Just keep your pen to yourself."

Dean picked up his pen and placed it securely inside the leather portfolio that held the pad of paper. "Just trying to be helpful," he countered with an acquiescent tone to his voice as he looked down at the table with a half-smile set on his face.

Lydia and the other people assembled looked toward the door to see two maintenance men arrive with the half-dozen folding chairs needed to seat the entire group of people. They worked rapidly and made an equally fast exit.

Minutes later, the now familiar squishing noises appeared, then a brief moment of quiet preempted the turn of the door knob as the department members straightened in their seats, waiting in expectation. Swaine stepped into the crowded conference room, and Macomber rose to greet him.

With an almost imperceptible nod, but without accepting Macomber's extended hand or seeking to make eye contact with anyone present, Swaine took his place in the empty seat at the head of the table.

"I'm Robert B. Swaine," he declared, loudly, as he proceeded to look at each successive face of those seated around the room. "I guess you've been told that I've been brought on board to oversee a large number of corporate departments, your own as well.

"That's not to say that you still won't be reporting to Macomber," he remarked in a patronizing manner. "But ultimately, your performance, or lack thereof, will ultimately be reported to me."

Swaine looked around the room for any sign of acknowledgement to his statement. There was none, so he continued.

"Let me explain it to you with a little story I picked up from one of my associates of the Jewish persuasion: A mohel—you know, the guy Jews have come into their homes to saw the foreskin off baby boys before they can object? Well, he saved all the remnants he removed over the years, in a huge jar of preservative. When he retired, he decided to have something done with these acquisitions to honor his long career."

Lydia felt her heart begin to race as she feared what was coming next. She glanced around the room to try to gauge other peoples' reaction but could not get a sense of how they were receiving this tirade. Even Christina and Dean seated on either side of her remained stone still, as if in shock. Karen Paulson had her head bowed and appeared to be focusing on a stain in the carpet. Goddard watched Swaine as if he were viewing a training film, and Williamsen actually looked as if he were enjoying himself.

Lydia's gaze fell on Macomber's face, which revealed a sadness he couldn't manage to disguise. Macomber also had placed his hand over his mouth in a vain attempt to suppress his nagging cough.

Swaine continued, "So he takes the jar of foreskins to a craftsman and asks him to create something of value in commemoration. The craftsman takes a long look at the jar, filled with thousands of mementos, and tells him that this job will be the challenge of his own career.

"A few weeks later, the Mohel gets a call from the craftsman to come down and collect his keepsake. When the Mohel arrives, the craftsman places a small box on the counter and removes a wallet. The Mohel says, 'With all the foreskins in that jar, the best you can do is a wallet?' The craftsman says, 'But this wallet is special. Think of what it's made of. All you have to do is rub the surface and BINGO, you have a briefcase.'"

Swaine slapped the table in appreciation of his own joke and roared. He settled back in his chair, looked around to see that no one else was laughing, and pitched his immense body forward again.

"Well I guess you folks don't get the point of my little story. What I notice in the background material I've been reading about you people is that, with few exceptions, you produce wallet-sized contributions to this company if you're so inclined, and you need a good deal of stroking to provide briefcase-sized work.

"Well, those days are over," he said abruptly. "From now on, you're going to have to produce those briefcases without the assistance of the emotional masturbation you've gotten from your leader, Macomber. The party's over, folks. In fact, I looked into canceling the Communicator's Conference I understand you're scheduled to attend next week. If it weren't already paid for with money the company can't recoup, you'd be back here at the ranch, earning an honest day's pay."

More silence.

"Questions?" he asked with amusement. When there was no response, he slapped the tabletop and said, "Meeting adjourned."

Swaine pushed himself away from the table, turned to Macomber, and said in a voice deliberately meant to be heard by all, "Macomber, I expected my office to be ready when I arrived. So what do I find? I find the chair for my desk wholly unacceptable for a man of my height, the light switch located where no one in their right mind would expect to find it, and the air filled with the worst smelling stench I ever smelled. Is that the way to welcome your new boss?"

Macomber looked up at Swaine's face, vigorously shook his head from side to side and brushed by him without uttering a word.

Lydia, along with Dean, Christina, and a few stragglers, watched Macomber head down the hallway, banging his left fist against the wall as he walked. Swaine brushed by the remaining department members and followed Macomber out. Lydia humbly admitted to herself that she admired Macomber's control but understood all too well that composure of that type would be impossible for any human being to maintain for any length of time. But they, she made mental note, are not dealing with a true human being. Rules without reasons, she thought, are meant to be broken.

<u>Chapter Eight</u>

The company cafeteria, known as "Mauser's Mess," was located directly across from the Corporate Relations Conference Room. Ernest Mauser, Manager of Food Services at Clearview Chemicals, ran his operation with all the elements of martial law. Although he had long ago retired from military service, there was a question as to whether the name came from his prior military affiliation or his manner of preparing food. Employees often laughed out loud at the confrontations that newcomers could expect from Mauser. If anyone questioned Mauser as to why there was no salad bar, Mauser would roughly reply, "Because we don't, that's why." And if the same person lacked the good sense to stop with that response and chose instead to belabor the point, Mauser relished the chance to rip off his chef's apron, throw it in the hapless victim's hands, and roar, "You think you can do this better? Put on the goddamned apron, you asshole, and show me!"

As the department members spilled out of their meeting with Swaine, they gravitated toward the lunchroom en masse and entered the cafeteria line. Christina spotted her favorite of Mauser's offerings: lentil soup.

"I'm not sure if I'll feel better with or without food after that meeting," Christina said to no one in particular as she ladled out a bowl of soup, placed it on her tray, and grabbed a handful of crackers.

The other members of their group casually selected their food, and Lydia, spotting an inviting piece of lemon meringue pie, placed the dessert on her tray before choosing a tuna salad platter that she felt required to eat before the pie.

The four friends found a square table by the floor-to-ceiling window that looked out on the snow-covered evergreens. Lydia, who sat next to Christina, placed her arm around her friend's shoulders and said, "Lighten up, Chris, and eat. Feeling better is not one of the alternatives we've been offered. Think of it this way: even those unfortunate souls on death row get a last meal."

"Whether we eat Mauser's outrageous crap or get fed to the lions as Swaine's proverbial wallets, we're dead meat." Goddard said quietly. Dean, who sat on the other side of Lydia, nodded in agreement.

"Listen guys," Handlesman said to the small group in the comforting voice he used to deliver his pitch as a lobbyist. "You make it seem as though we are not going to survive this situation. Don't lose sight of the fact that he is only one man, and one without a following. There is only so much damage he can do without support from within the ranks, and support from within is something he doesn't know how to harness. Trust me, he's not going to get very far with the attitude he displayed today. He might have Wainwright fooled for now, but I guarantee that he can't sustain that kind of allegiance in order to do what he wants to do here. He'll be stopped long before that."

Goddard looked surprised at Handlesman's confidence. "How can you possibly project that kind of outcome, Dean? You know the man comes equipped with a hit man's history."

Lydia quietly interjected, "And an iceman's heart."

Dean vehemently shook his head from side to side. "You've simply lost sight of this company's culture. You know that one man won't be permitted to change the way a company with a history of respect for individuals does business, at least not for long. I've seen people like him come and go in other places I've worked," Dean said quietly and with conviction. "It's only a matter of time. We just have to be patient and do our jobs as well as we have always done them." He shrugged his shoulders and added, "then wait."

Linda Spear

Chapter Nine

The foursome did not dawdle over lunch as they occasionally did on a relatively slow day. With their meals completed far earlier than usual, they headed back to the department enclave. When they rounded the corner of the corridor that led to their offices in Office Building One, all eyes fell on the office of R.B. Swaine.

It was not hard to note through the beveled glass that separated the walls from the door that all lights were on; a figure was behind the desk, but the door was fully closed.

As Lydia began to enter her office, Dean suddenly took hold of her arm and muttered, "I'm not ready to get back to my desk yet. I need some air."

"But it's bitter cold out there," Lydia replied in surprise. "And it's icy as hell on the walkways."

"I need the air," he replied assertively, "and you could use a walk to clear your head too."

Lydia nodded, and without hesitation reached into her closet and drew out her coat and boots. "Just let me get these on first, and I'll join you at your office." Dean didn't move. "Don't you want to get your coat?"

"I'm afraid that if I go back into my office, I'll get trapped by the ringing phones and the other shit that's waiting for me. Oh, what the hell," he said in annoyance, and headed down the hallway.

I wonder what's eating at him all of a sudden, Lydia thought as she tugged on her boots. Probably just another case of Mauser food poisoning. She nodded, laughed to herself, slipped on her coat, and wrapped a wooly scarf around her neck as she followed him down the hall.

Dean stepped quickly into his office and did not even bother to turn on the overhead light. He reached into the closet, pulled out his overcoat, doubled back, and took hold of Lydia's arm as she stepped up beside him in the hallway. Together they left the building.

Side by side, they gingerly stepped onto the flagstone walkway that separated one building from the next and walked into the wooded trails that surrounded the complex.

Lydia turned halfway toward Dean, stopped, and asked him, "What's wrong? You seemed fine at lunch, but now you're obviously in a different state of mind."

"To tell you the truth, Lydia, I'm more concerned about that bozo than I'd like to admit to the others." He pulled a pair of soft black leather gloves from his pockets and carefully placed them on each hand as he talked.

"It occurred to me as we passed his closed door when we came back from lunch. I haven't seen his door open all morning. That, in itself, means a lot. It will certainly mean that he's not, literally or figuratively, open to communication with a department chock full of communicators.

"Funny," he added with a wry look on his face. "I'd like to think that Clearview's rational thinkers will see the light long before our pal Swaine can do any damage, but I can't help worrying. Swaine's obviously not going to make any attempt to get to know us and find out our existing value to this firm. If he's come here with a prearranged plan, changes could be made before we have any chance to show him that he's barking up the wrong tree."

Dean took Lydia's hand and added, "This guy Swaine must be taken very seriously. Remember, Wainwright knows exactly what he was hired to do. If he wasn't brought in to cut back and streamline the company with extreme prejudice, he would not have been hired in the first place."

He added almost to himself, "It could mean all of our jobs. I have a wife to support, and she's itching to have kids soon."

"Yes, and I have condo and car payments," said Lydia lightly, in an effort to improve Dean's perspective.

He looked at her and smiled as he said, "I guess I'm forgetting that little black convertible of yours needs fuel, too."

Lydia put her arm through his, and pulled him along. "I'm certainly not negating any of what you've said, Dean, at lunch or privately to me now, but I think we've all got first-day jitters. He's bound to create problems, but most of us have proven track records. I think we've got to keep our distance and let our work speak for itself. Wainwright knows our capabilities.

"What I'm most curious about," she added, "is whether he'll make an appearance at the Communicator's Conference next week. He sure came down hard on that issue."

Dean answered immediately. "I'd bet on it," he said staunchly. "That guy would never pass up an opportunity to again condemn what he believes to be a recreational venture. But," he added, "It would certainly be to our advantage if he comes at a time when all of the data we expect to compile in the first two days is projected and analyzed on the third day. Maybe Macomber has already arranged for him to come, knowing that he could not ignore our findings if he is a captive audience."

The two walked silently for several minutes more, both seemingly aware of the quiet forest area in which they hiked. At lunchtime, during good weather, the trails that surrounded the chemical company complex were often replete with other employees anxious to take advantage of the tranquil setting. The polar vortex, plus the snow and ice, dissuaded most people from traversing the area on this day, choosing to wait until sometime closer to spring.

Lydia shivered as a gust of frigid air threatened to knock her off her feet. Dean placed his arm around her shoulders and pulled her close to him.

"You don't have to do that," she said to him. "I'm not that cold or fragile."

"I know," he replied, and hugged her tighter. "I just felt like showing you how much your friendship means to me. Whenever I need to see things clearly, I know I can look to you for advice, and as usual you didn't prove me wrong."

Lydia turned to face Dean and placed her head on his chest. He rested his check on the top of her head, placed both arms around her, and they stood, molded tightly together for several minutes more.

As she looked up at him, Dean took her face in his hands and kissed her mouth, sensually, without question as to the intent of the gesture.

"I take it that's your way to warm me up," Lydia said softly. Dean backed away as he laughed at her response.

"You're something special, Lydia Barrett," he stated with considerable admiration in his voice.

"Something special."

Chapter Ten

Karen Paulson was the first to follow Daniel J. Macomber out of the eleven o'clock meeting held in the Corporate Relations Conference Room. She was also the first to watch him bang his fist into the walls of the corridor in a staccato rhythm as he headed directly back to his office.

Even before Macomber had the chance to sit down at his desk and extract a straw from the first drawer on the right, Karen was standing in his doorway, waiting to be heard.

Macomber sensed her presence even before she placed a preemptory knock on the doorframe.

"What do you want, Karen?"

"Dan, I need to talk with you about Swaine and the Communicator's Conference." She continued without taking a breath. "I want to know what you are going to do to prove the need for the conference to him. I need to know, Dan. I'm the coordinator of this effort, and I'll be damned if I'm going to let all the work I've put in go down the tubes because you haven't explained the rationale to him."

Without asking, Karen seated herself in one of the chairs before Macomber's desk. She leaned forward and placed her folded arms on the front of his desk as she waited for an answer.

Macomber looked helplessly at the woman before him. Her carefully made-up face was set in the familiar confrontational manner that was hers alone, and even her softly highlighted shoulder-length hair did not appear to be giving an inch.

"It's lunchtime, Karen. Why don't we just order up some sandwiches, and we'll talk this over calmly." The words were Macomber's first attempt to mollify the angry woman.

"I'm not hungry, Dan," she replied curtly. "I just want to know why you didn't defend me and my arrangements for this conference at today's meeting. I'm going to be seen as the creator of a big waste of corporate residual."

Macomber had become used to Karen's tirades. Several years back, when she believed that her annual raise was not sufficient, she raced over to Human Resources to learn the average percentage for all corporate employees in the tri-state area at her level.

When Lydia was promoted shortly thereafter to the manager's position she currently held, Karen went straight to Macomber and demanded to know what was still required of her to get a raise in title and financial compensation. And, when those requirements were met, she insisted that he establish a timeframe for her advancement to that level. The promotion came three months later. Karen Paulson, Macomber thought tiredly, was certainly the proverbial "squeaky wheel."

"Karen, I'll do my best to inform Swaine of the value of the conference, but you have to admit that it's going to be an uphill battle—one that I'm not sure I can win because I'm the one who arranged for the symposium in the first place, not you."

The angry woman's body language told Macomber her reaction to his placation, seconds before she spoke again.

"You're not going let him show up before the final meeting, are you?"

"If he shows up before that and gets his impressions before all the data is in," he said hurriedly, "what can I do? Tie him to his office chair?"

Karen shook with rage and yelled at her boss, "Well, then stop him, damn it. Do whatever you need to make sure he doesn't come to the conference before we can pull together all the final results and prove the worth of the whole damn thing. He's screwing up my future."

As he listened to her latest invective, he thought to himself that early retirement might not be so bad after all.

Chapter Eleven

The queen-sized bed in the Handlesman house was stacked high with clothing, piles of papers, and a large binder. They were ready to be placed in the open suitcase. Dean's briefcase lay nearby.

He picked up folded sweaters and shirts and thought about what would match yet still fit in the suitcase. As he lay them down in the carry-all, he gave each some thought and picked them up again. He considered all the other items as he mixed and matched.

"You act like you are packing for a weekend at the White House," Patti Handlesman said as she watched her husband mull over his choices. "You've been to these corporate conferences so many times before, and I've never seen you so engrossed in what you were bringing."

Dean stopped for a minute, and in that moment of distraction he turned his head in his wife's direction.

"This one is a special event, Patti. I'm not only going to a national conference with all the corporate affairs people at Clearview, but I need to dress for the evening events as well as for the consideration of senior management."

He continued to pack and added, "Do you want me to get the promotion I've been waiting for, or are you just going to ask me idiotic questions as to why I'm being so careful about what I bring?"

Dean turned back to the heaps of clothing and drew the empty luggage closer to him on the bed to continue loading the clothing inside.

Patti, Dean's wife of three years, stood nearby and watched as her husband's full attention was on the project at hand.

"Well, can I take some of the clothing off the bed that you are not packing and put them away?" she asked quietly, as she crawled onto the empty part of the bed and slowly began to undress.

Dean looked at her and snapped, "Can't you just leave me alone with this? I know what I want to take with me, and you don't. So just go into another room, and keep yourself occupied, please."

"Bastard," she hissed. She ran out of the bedroom and into the kitchen, where she opened the refrigerator and grabbed a cold bottle of chardonnay. Directly above the closest counter she reached for a goblet from the rack, poured herself a full glass, and took it into the living room, where she plopped onto the couch to begin consuming her drink.

It was one in the afternoon.

"Damn, you son of a bitch," she muttered, knowing he wasn't listening. Nor was she speaking loud enough to be heard. "Why can't you even have a civil conversation with me when you are leaving me for almost a week?"

Patti tossed back the wine and went into to the kitchen for more. When she came back to the living room, she noticed Dean coming toward her from their bedroom with a scowl on his face.

"You're drinking already? It's not even close to cocktail hour. I could smell the booze all the way back in the bedroom. Have you been slugging that stuff down all day?"

Patti drank some more and slammed the glass down on the coffee table.

"I just began to drink the wine when you threw me out of the room," she said angrily. "Why are you treating me this way?"

Dean had the suitcase and his briefcase in each hand and put them down on the floor so he could motion with both hands for Patti to come to him.

"I'm so sorry, baby," he said soothingly. "I just got carried away with what I need to do for this meeting, and I lost sight of your feelings in the process."

He hugged her and kissed the top of her blond curly head. "There's a lot going on at the site regarding laboratory accidents. There are chemical odors floating about the connecting buildings, and that's a big OSHA problem that we have to fix soon or it will cost the company millions in compensatory fees, and that will be hard for me to explain to the folks below the Beltway.

"We also have a new head boss of all the corporate groups, who may be here to offload those of us who he considers unessential. I can't afford to look unnecessary."

Patti, who stood a foot shorter than her husband, quickly wrapped her arms around his waist and said, "I understand how hard it is for you to deal with stuff that's not your issue, honey. All you want to do is your own work and come home to find some peace. I didn't mean to upset you," she said softly.

Dean held her tightly, feeling very ashamed of the way he had treated her.

"I'm naked and drunk," she said to Dean, with emphasis on the 'naked' as she started to pull at his shirt. Patti swiftly worked to undress her husband as she pulled him to the couch with all the effort she could muster.

As he moved forward, he stumbled forward over the low-slung coffee table and landed on top of his wife. They giggled as his clothing came off, and Patti continued to wrap herself around her husband in a way he could never resist.

In short order, Patti made love to her husband.

It took some time before he began to realize that his trip across the coffee table had left his knees aching and bruised.

Patti hastily got up from the couch and ran to the bathroom to get some Aleve, knowing it would reduce the inflammation and pain he felt. She also got a bottle of cold Aquafina from the fridge to wash down the pills.

Dean stood up to pull on his clothing and take the medicine.

"Thank you, honey. Thanks for loving me," he said with little enthusiasm.

What he did dwell on was that Patti was an understanding wife with a loving soul. What he couldn't tell her was that there was more to plan for at the conference than his work.

*

Karen looked closely in her bathroom mirror and delicately touched her face. Did the red splotches caused by the latest Botox injections still show? How long did Dr. Rosen say it would take for them to disappear? And the shadows around her eyes looked worse. Was it because the night before had been virtually sleepless? Maybe it was time to get cosmetic surgery done beneath her eyes and more work done on her nose.

Oh well. That's what makeup and Dr. Rosen were for. "And I won't forget that I'll come through this fine," she said out loud, although the only one within hearing distance was Domino, her cat.

Karen's files and charts were carefully wrapped in bubble wrap and boxes, awaiting their use at the conference. She worked tirelessly on the preparation for this event and the effort showed.

Throughout the day, she would periodically pack and unpack the materials to gaze upon them, just one more time. Another glance at her work product would only help her to be certain that no mistake had been made and her future was secure.

"Domino, by the end of this conference, that jerk Swaine will be forced to recognize my skills. There won't be any way he'll think to yank my job out from under me. Anyone can tell how good I am at organization and delivery. Unlike Lydia, who sits on her ass all day commanding people to do her bidding. She thinks she's getting away with it, but I bet he knows full well that she doesn't deserve the praise she gets. All she does is give away those gooey sweet things she eats at her desk. I, on the other hand, work hard and don't provide handouts."

Domino turned and slowly walked away, wholly uninterested in her owner's words.

*

Christina Benderhoff was a completely crestfallen woman. *Is that monster going to fire me at the conference or wait until we are back at the office where everyone in the department will hear him and see me fall apart?*

She ruminated on this crisis as she stood before her closet. *What should I wear to get fired? Ah, purple. It's a prominent color of death,* she thought. *Should I carry lilies too?*

Christina had no hope. Her life as far as she could imagine had gone down the drain with her tears.

Besides the purple dress and heels to match, she chose black. In her carefully packed suitcase lay black slacks, black pullovers, a black dress, black flats, and black sneakers for her morning jog around the facility.

All suitable for this occasion, which I will consider a wake for my lost job. Maybe I'll just jog right off a cliff.

I wish I was Lydia; she's got it all. No one steps on her toes. I don't even think that Swaine punished her for anything…at least not so far. Wait 'til he hears her presentation at the conference. Maybe he'll take his wrath out on her then.

Hell, she's my best friend at that awful place. Why would I want to wish her the same bad stuff that's coming down on me?

Without thought, Christina hurried to her kitchen and carefully wrapped six cranberry-orange muffins to eat at the conference. She hoped they wouldn't get stale despite the intricate way she encased them.

What if I lose my job and can't afford to buy what I need? What if I can't find another job in the New York area? What if people who interview me see how depressed I am and believe I'm not hirable? Scattered thoughts of annihilation ran through her mind. Her own annihilation, of course.

*

Lydia hastily rummaged through her closet to see what didn't need dry cleaning. She only really needed one special outfit for her presentation on Tuesday morning that dealt with the media and its effect on chemical companies. There was no end to the questions those information mongers asked regarding chemical spills and other noxious issues related to the industry.

Other than what was needed for this presentation, more casual clothing was called for, courtesy of Karen's pointed email messages to all who would attend. Casual clothing was something that she could manage to dig up instantly.

So one suit for the first evening's banquet dinner, a skirt with matching sweaters, pants to go with everything, and two simple dresses were all that she decided were necessary.

Karen—what a wise ass. The woman could not get past her own importance. I wonder what she was packing. A loaded pistol? The thought brought a smile to her face.

Lydia knew well how much effort Karen made to be recognized for her work and her good looks. I guess one could say that she works at her beauty as well. They seemed to go hand in hand. Although Lydia found it funny to think about that subject, the guys at the office never seemed to be interested in Karen. She was too artificial, or they were just plain scared of her. In fact, Randy once said that she looked like she always had a rod up her ass. My feelings exactly, Lydia thought.

As she finished packing her clothes and toiletries, she thought about Dean. One thing she decided was that there would be no perfume in her carryall bag. "I'm just not the type," she said out loud, "and neither is he to care for it."

*

"Randy, you've got umpteen shirts, and not one of them fits you properly anymore," Diane, his wife, moaned as she watched her husband go through shirt after shirt in an effort to find one that covered his ever-expanding waistline.

"Honey," Diane added kindly, "You're going to have to take this weight off. Otherwise, you'll have to buy all new clothes."

At the very thought of spending money on clothing, Randy quickly nodded in agreement at Diane's suggestion.

"But Di," he whined, "I have to get through this nonsense conference before I can concentrate on myself. There's just too much at stake for me to spend my working hours counting calories."

"Don't count calories, Randy. Just eat carefully, and stay away from the fattening desserts. That will be a good start."

Randy nodded remorsefully and made a mental note to try. After all, Diane really did have his best interests at heart. She didn't even know how tough life had gotten at work with R.B. Swaine in the mix.

The last thing I have to worry about is my waist, he thought. If Swaine doesn't feel I'm providing enough input for the company to reduce global warming, bad air quality, and animal testing, my clothing won't be my biggest problem.

*

Macomber worried continuously as he placed his finely tailored suits in a hanging bag and his shirts, sweaters, and underwear in a carryall.

"The rest of them may want to be casual," he said to Fiona, but I'm not going to let Swaine see me as anything but the appropriately dressed executive.

Fiona finished ironing his handkerchiefs and laid them carefully on top of the shirts and sweaters already packed in the full bag.

"This is going to be hard on you, sweetie," she said to her anxious husband. "I know that it feels as though Swaine has you tied up in knots, but people like him don't last long in a corporate environment. They move on, and you know it. Try to keep that in mind as you go through these next few days."

Macomber looked lovingly at Fiona. She had been through many near-disasters while he worked at the chemical company as federal and local laws constantly changed and people's concerns increased. Swaine would have to be dealt with soon, or this could be his own swan song.

As the head of the public relations arm of the company, it was Macomber's responsibility to deal with all issues brought forth by the media and the public. They always needed to be answered directly with changing mission statements.

And he had provided those statements. His regular commentary concerning the environment and global warning had been on point and reflective of what the public wanted and needed to hear.

"I know, my sweet darling," he said. "But this problem is bigger than a mission statement. It may be more than I can handle with any simple report I make to the public."

And what about Fiona? She was used to the finer things in life. She might have to learn to do something infinitely more important than ironing my handkerchiefs.

Linda Spear

*

Gunnar Williamsen didn't worry about what he packed or straightening up his apartment. Why should he? The routine stuff that these stiffs would do and talk about was old school for him.

As Manager of Art Services, he had no interest in the process of streamlining his own work that moved along in the direction that suited him. And he had his own schedule set out for him.

Without a thought in his mind, he threw his everyday clothing into a worn-out duffle bag, knowing he didn't need to stand before anyone to be judged.

Leaving his Spartan-like one-bedroom apartment that was on the second floor of a duplex, he walked out of his front door, wallet in pocket, duffle underneath his arm, keys in hand, and slid into his Saab to move onto the conference center. He never looked back.

Chapter Twelve

Sunday, January 5

The East Forge Conference Center was located exactly four miles northeast of Clearview Chemicals. The complex of meeting rooms, lounges, hotel accommodations, and banquet rooms were positioned so conveniently that participants of any conference scheduled by Clearview Chemicals, or any of the other corporations also headquartered nearby, could be as close to work as they were to their homes.

East Forge had been Clearview's conference center of choice for many years. Charles B. Wainwright, in fact, had become so enamored of the center's luxurious, perfectly heated indoor swimming pool, that whenever he attended meetings at the center, he routinely swam each morning before he dressed and again every evening before he returned to his room to sleep.

Employees who attended the same meeting and chose to swim at the same time were often surprised by the sight of their CEO flailing away through a choppy butterfly stroke.

Wainwright, however, was not expected to attend the Communicator's Conference scheduled for the second week in January at East Forge.

On tap for the first three days of that week, the attendees were the writers, editors, community relations, public relations, and government affairs people employed at the twenty-one Clearview locations nationwide, who conveyed company business to other employees and the outside world.

The group convened yearly to share information, discuss issues, and get to know each other better. The result, it was heartily agreed, was a better-informed workforce and a public familiar with what Clearview Chemicals believed important for consumers to know.

Karen Paulson had worked continuously to make all the logistical plans and develop this year's conference into what she referred to as a "quasi town meeting."

Her objective, she was quick to tell anyone who was willing to listen, was to encourage the large group of communicators to draft a plan that would eliminate unnecessary repetitions that could effectively be done by one person for many.

One of many examples was the vast amount of paperwork required to keep a bureaucracy afloat. Newly developed software, she firmly considered, would offer up easy-to-follow forms geared to reduce the number of hands that touched them. This idea would be offered up to the entire assemblage on the last day of the conference.

Karen recognized the value of her preparedness. With encouragement, other employees would step forward and offer to undertake the simplification of the other processes.

She was even ready to introduce a new slogan, one she believed would guarantee cooperation among her colleagues. "Working Together with Vitality," she repeated to herself. How could they not be enthused with her concept?

She contemplated the look that R.B. Swaine would have on his face when he recognized that she was wholly responsible for the dramatic changes she planned to initiate among the large group of employees. He had to see her as a cut above the rest, she mused, and then, in another daydream, she casually moved on to thoughts of the going-away party for Macomber she'd be sure to applaud.

Karen, dressed in a muted navy blue light wool suit with a crisp cotton long-sleeved white blouse that featured large pearl buttons and cufflinks, positioned herself in front of the registration desk on the Sunday afternoon at the onset of the conference. There she waited patiently for each participant to arrive. As she moved from side to side in an effort to look active, she grasped the lengthy list of employees' names accompanied by the travel plans for each of those who journeyed from a distance.

Karen had carefully arranged for company-chartered limousines to pick up those conference participants at various times throughout the afternoon as planes landed at Westchester County, LaGuardia, and Kennedy from locations across the country.

As she undertook the role of a singular welcoming committee, she had to admit, even to herself, that her greeting was a shade officious. But, what the hell, she thought as she waited for the conference attendees by the registration desk. She relished the opportunity to be seen and noticed for the first time in as far back as she wished to remember.

"Randy, how *are* you?" she said unctuously, as Randall Goddard, dressed in chinos and a tightfitting red and green Christmas crewneck sweater, obviously a gift of the holiday season, approached the desk.

Goddard was plainly taken aback by her unexpected cordiality. Karen Paulson, he knew, was not one for small talk. A quick cut to the chase—that's her, he always thought when he watched her maneuver through department groupings.

Randy smiled and looked somewhat quizzically at her mannequin-like stance by the registration desk. The other two members of the registration staff were seated at the adjacent table where the conference schedules were placed. They watched Goddard's actions in response to Karen's directions with giddy amusement.

"Just let them know that you're here," she instructed Randy, "and they'll check you right through. I've completed all the preliminary details, and don't forget—dinner at the Converse House at seven."

Goddard filled out the requisite forms at the table as he observed Karen working the crowd that queued up behind him. He shook his head in exasperation as he grabbed his overnight bag and walked toward the exit of the conference center's administrative building.

As he opened the door, he turned to hear Karen Paulson again solicitously call out in the direction of the front entrance, "Dean, how *are* you?"

__Chapter Thirteen__

Dinner at the Converse House at the center of the grounds was called for seven on Sunday evening. Although casual attire was permitted throughout the daytime events, employees were requested to dress in clothing "suitable for an evening event." To Lydia, this meant her black suede suit with a cropped jacket, a claret-red long sleeve silk blouse, suede open-toe slingback heels, and black mesh stockings.

As she looked at herself in the mirror that lay flush to the wall next to the front door of her room, she tugged at the skirt that she decided, on second thought, might be too short for a work-related event. She considered spiking the top of her layered silky black hair, which fell in uniform lengths to her shoulders, and then erred on the safe side of conservatism as she brushed the bangs forward and the sides back.

"Oh, the hell with it," she said out loud. "I look respectable." Lydia then remembered her phone conversation with Christina, just minutes before.

With a case of mounting nerves, Christina called Lydia to assure herself that she had brought the proper clothing.

"I really don't know if what I'm wearing for this dinner is too dressy," she explained with a tremulous voice. Lydia recalled the clothing that she mentioned and knew that impeccably groomed Christina had chosen the right dress, but she railed at the unnecessary insecurity her friend displayed.

"For Christ's sake, Christina, it's only a fucking corporate dinner. You've been to so many of them before."

There was silence at the other end of the line. Lydia heard the barest of sighs and knew that she had offended her friend with the burst of insensitivity.

"I didn't mean to get annoyed with you, Chris," she told her friend. "It's just that you always look a lot more put together than almost anyone else, and you don't have to worry about that dress. I'm sure it's fine."

Lydia could visualize Christina threading her fingers through her hair as she held onto the phone with the other hand, and thought about how carefully Christina prepared for every day—down to the fresh cranberry-orange muffin she ate for breakfast.

"Just put the phone down, brush your hair, and have one of your muffins," she said placatingly, "and meet me in the lounge bar at six. I'll treat you to a dirty martini. Oh, don't eat a muffin. It's too close to dinnertime."

"How did you know that I brought along muffins?" Christina asked softly, with unmistakable surprise.

Lydia shrieked with laughter. "I was only kidding you. Christ, you actually brought those little fuckers with you?"

There was no answer on the other end of the line.

"Dean's going to love this one, Chris."

Dean, in fact, had called Lydia's room shortly after arriving at the conference center at three. It was the first time the two had spoken since the walk they had taken on the day following the holiday week.

"When can we get together, just the two of us," he asked her.

"Remember," he told her, "We need to make time to talk."

How could she forget, she asked herself, as she tugged at her skirt?

She reminded herself, as she had in as many days when she recalled their conversation after his kiss on the bitter cold day following New Year's, that Dean was not a free man.

"You're married," she had said perfunctorily, eyes straight ahead.

"You noticed," Dean replied, and pulled on her hand. Lydia allowed herself to smile. "I know that I shouldn't be allowing myself to think about you as much as I do," he said as his tone became serious again. "But I spend more time talking about things with you than I do with Patti."

Lydia shook her head and raised her hand to his arm to interrupt him, and he again took hold of her fingers as he continued to speak. "It's not your fault, and it's not mine either," he said softly, looking toward the ground. "It's no one's fault. I just can't help thinking about you—and caring for you. I've known you too long to look at you as a passing interest."

Lydia watched his thought processes play across his face. She knew them well.

"We'll have time to discuss this during the free time at the conference next week," he stated resolutely, as if to release the emotional pull that kept them in place on the path in the woods.

"What time? You know that they keep you going at full tilt during those conferences. At least they better," she said. "As Swaine has so aptly reminded us, we better be ready to go there to earn an honest day's pay."

"We'll find the time." Dean spoke softly. He kissed her again quickly, and as he led the way to the opening of the thicket onto the flagstone terrace that led to Office Building One, he dropped her hand and quickened his pace. Lydia heard him repeat, "We'll find the time."

Chapter Fourteen

Dinner at the Converse House was renowned for its simple elegance. Conference goers from past years continued to marvel at the stained glass windows that adorned the gothic exterior of the banquet area of the complex.

Once the permanent residence of the Converse family, who were directly linked to settlers from the Revolutionary era, Converse House served as the centerpiece for the additional buildings that were erected at a later date on the property. Sold by the remaining descendants to developers in the early seventies, the property became known as the East Forge Conference Center. The mix of post-Revolutionary architecture and a reasonable facsimile of a prior age carried over to the additional structures, which were webbed together by flagstone paths and graced on each side by evergreen hedges, and gave the Center a sense of history and permanence.

The only building not in keeping with the period architecture was Cromwell House. Designed with ultra-modern amenities, it was used solely for sleeping accommodations and the comfort of the guests. Built to accommodate over 300 people at a time, the low slung, two-story, modern structure was accessible from many different entrances. As the last building to be constructed for its current purpose, the designers concentrated on what they believed to be of primary importance to overnight guests—safety and convenience. The overall appearance of the Center itself, however, held wide appeal for the many corporations in the area, which were happy to entertain clients and book international events at the site.

A fire was roaring in the stone hearth of the large anteroom in Converse House at six when Lydia, with her coat carelessly thrown over her shoulders, entered the main house.

Although the dining rooms that extended past the foyer were prepared for dinner, several visitors relaxed in the overstuffed chairs surrounding the fire. Lydia headed directly to the lounge found in the basement area, stopping only to hang her coat in the unattended check room to the left of the stairway that led below.

Already familiar with the logistics of the facility, as were many return visitors, she was pleased to see a small group of her colleagues gathered around the cocktail tables that circled the mahogany bar.

Settled among them was Christina, dressed in a purple boucle dress. Around her neck were a string of pink pearls with matching studs in her ears. She looked up in anticipation as she saw Lydia approach and whispered quickly, "Do I look ridiculous?"

Lydia concealed her annoyance over her friend's preoccupation. "I've seen you in this before, and you look as good in it as you did then," she replied. "But why are you so concerned about how you look now?"

Christina gulped the remainder the martini she had ordered beforehand and motioned with her index finger for Lydia to come closer. The nearby waiter took the motion to mean that she wanted another drink.

"I think Swaine is coming to the agenda segment of the meeting after dinner tonight."

Lydia looked at Christina with suspicion. Where did you hear that?" she asked in earnest. "And why should that matter so much to you?" Her voice became louder with unconcealed annoyance. "Swaine doesn't give a rat's ass about any of us. He'd never notice if the entire group of us were facing him buck-naked. Actually…" she considered, "he might notice that. Nah," she said as much to herself as she did to her friend.

"Shhh," cautioned Christina. "If I knew it would get you going on a diatribe, I wouldn't have said anything. Just forget I even said it," she added petulantly. She turned away and signaled to the waiter, pointing to her empty glass.

"Make it two," called out Lydia as she sat down across from her friend.

"Are you sure you can take my preoccupation?" Christina remarked offhandedly.

"Will you cut this out," Lydia answered without rancor.

"I don't want to fight with you. I just don't understand why you are so worried about this man. He hasn't had time to do anything yet that should shake you up like this."

"Oh, yes he has," Christina said quietly, as she took another long gulp of her second martini. "He called me into his office last Friday to talk about the final draft of the Annual Report."

Lydia interrupted Christina to say, "That's great work that you did. He must have told you that."

"Oh, no he didn't," Christina responded. Tears began to well up in her eyes. "He told me that the writing was—how did he phrase it? 'Pedestrian,' and the marketing thrust was, in his words, 'weak and insipid.'"

"It's just the opinion of that slimy butcher, Chris. It's meant to keep you under his thumb, and so far he's succeeding."

Lydia grasped her friend's shoulders and shook them.

"Remember, I proofed the report when it was in the pre-print stages, so I know it was damned good. Why didn't you tell me this before?" she said with real anger directed solely at herself as she thought about how rough she had been on the woman.

"It's more than just his opinion, Lydia. He told me that he was going to shelve the entire piece of work and hire an outside consultant to rewrite it in the manner he says it deserves. You know what that means? The damned thing was budgeted for last year, and if it's redone, that means I will have spent almost two hundred thousand dollars of the company's money for nothing." The volume of her voice increased and she added, "You know what that means don't you?"

Lydia put her hand on Chris' arm and tried to calm her. "If I don't talk him out of it, I'll probably get fired for wasting the corporation's money, as well as doing a shitty job."

Lydia, subdued by her friend's account, asked, "Can you challenge Swaine on his decision? How about defending the figure for what was spent on that project that is not allocated in this year's budget? Does he realize that he can't simply cancel an already-produced piece of printed material without consulting Wainwright and the other members of senior management? They were the ones who wholly approved your final copy in the first place."

"That's the problem," Christina answered. Tears now freely flowed down her pinched face. "Swaine met with Wainwright last week—in fact, on the day that he chewed out the whole department, remember? Swaine said that Wainwright told him that it was his call. HIS CALL! I'm going to be out of a job, Lydia, unless I can convince him to back off."

Lydia no longer attempted to argue. She knew it was a hopeless cause.

*

Shortly before seven, the bulk of the group assembled at the entry to Converse House's dining room. Lydia, having nursed the one martini, guided a heavily sedated Christina to the doorway.

Dean, in a dark grey suit, sitting in one of the overstuffed chairs by the fireside, looked at the two women with curiosity. There, before him, was a glazed Christina, supported by the arm of her anxious friend.

"Get an early start, Chris?"

Lydia shot him a cautious look, and he moved quickly to Chris' other side, taking her other arm.

"What happened to her?" he said as he turned to Lydia, whispering his concern. Lydia just shook her head and smiled at some colleagues as they led Christina away from the gathering crowd.

"She's loaded."

Christina began to cry again as Dean and Lydia dragged her outside to the frigid air.

"She had four Grey Goose martinis in an hour," Lydia told him. "I tried to stop her, but she was dead set on getting loose."

"Loose is one thing," Dean laughed, "but she's not functional."

"I think it's best if we take her back to her room, even if she has to miss the dinner. She'll do herself more harm if she goes into that banquet room in this state. We can tell anyone who asks that she's not feeling well."

Dean agreed, and together, they slowly guided the unsteady Christina back to the Cromwell House, through the sliding glass door, and down the low-lit hotel corridor.

Lydia slipped Christina's purse off her shoulder to search for her room key, which was perched at the top of the clutter found inside the bag.

"Room 118. She's staying here on the first floor," a relieved Lydia told Dean. "We won't have to get her by as many people on the stairway and have to try to explain this."

"We're close to her room," he saw as they directed Christina down the hall. "I'll hold her up while you open the door and turn on the lights." Dean shifted Christina's weight in his direction, and Lydia moved a few feet ahead to Room 118 to quickly unlock the door.

"I'm going to be sick," came the feeble voice of the wretchedly drunk Christina as they entered the room. Lydia quickly led her to the bathroom and shut the door behind them.

"Real bright, Chris, real bright," she mumbled, mainly to herself as her friend relieved herself of the martinis, a cranberry-orange muffin, and the few pretzels she had consumed along the way.

After helping Christina to wash her face and brush her teeth, Lydia opened the bathroom door to find that Dean had turned down the covers of the bed and closed the drapes.

They removed Christina's shoes, though they made no attempt to remove Christina's purple silk dress, before they lowered their friend onto the bed, leaving one light lit for her safety.

"Sleep it off, Chris," said Dean as he carefully pulled the covers up to her chin. "We'll make your excuses, don't worry." Dean gently placed his hand on Christina's head to comfort her. She nodded faintly and mouthed the word, thanks.

Lydia, moved by his gesture of care, took his hand as she placed Christina's room key on the night table next to her traveling alarm clock.

"Do you think she'll see it here?" she whispered to Dean.

"She really can't miss it," he replied as he pulled her toward the door. "We've got to get back to that dinner, fast. This is not the right time or place to make a late entrance."

The two rushed back down the corridor and out the same exit they entered. Without the coat she had left behind at the Converse House coat check room, she instinctively wrapped her arms around her shoulders, and Dean reached an arm around hers to warm her. Lydia abruptly pulled away. Dean stopped, and Lydia turned to see why.

"Listen, I need to hold you tonight," he insisted.

"Later, I promise," she answered.

Dean reached into his suit jacket pocket for his key and placed it in her hand.

"Room 136. Meet me as soon as you can leave the group after the dinner. I'll join you in my room a little bit after I see you leave the banquet room. You know that we can't leave together."

She nodded in agreement, and felt her heart quicken as she met his gaze.

Chapter Fifteen

Although most of the dinner guests were clustered together by the time Dean and Lydia arrived for the second time at the dining room, there were still a few people in the final stages of table-hopping before the actual event began.

Lydia entered the banquet room first and found a seat at a table of colleagues from the Shreveport, Louisiana, corporate site. Already familiar with a large number of the people seated there, she picked up a copy of the three-and-a-half-day conference schedule left at each place setting and fell into an easy conversation with Renee Trottier, the woman who held the corresponding position to Lydia's at the Shreveport site.

She noticed from the corner of her eye that Dean had placed himself with the group from Michigan—one of the major stops on his route throughout the country in his role as a lobbyist.

Determined only to do what was required of her at the conference, and now in addition to protect Christina from excess scrutiny, Lydia launched into conversation with Renee and the others at her table.

"Where's Christina?" asked Renee during their conversation.

"She came here today with the beginnings of a migraine," Lydia lied easily, having already prepared the story in her mind. "By the time we were ready to gather for dinner, she couldn't hold her head up any longer, and I helped her to her room." Renee looked sympathetic as Lydia continued, "I know she had her migraine medication with her so I believe that she'll be fine by tomorrow morning."

A clinking of silverware against crystal disturbed their conversation as Dan Macomber mounted the podium at the dais.

"Welcome, everyone, to the Fifth Annual Communicator's

Linda Spear

Conference. Does it seem like that long to you veterans out there that we agreed to meet once a year to talk about what mutually concerns us as chemical company communicators?"

Macomber recognized a group from the Boston, Massachusetts, site and waved in their direction.

"One of these days I'm going to get up to see you guys to do Saint Paddy's Day with you." A wave of applause was heard from their direction.

"Before we begin to map out our agenda, I want to publically thank Karen Paulson of the corporate headquarters for undertaking the mammoth job of arranging this conference. She put in incredibly long hours arranging the agenda you see before you that will certainly pique your interest and hopefully draw upon your skills as communicators to provide valuable input to the group as a whole.

"Karen, stand up and take a bow."

As Karen was dressed elegantly in a white wool dress, she was obviously pleased with the acknowledgement and stood in place at her table. Macomber began to clap, and the crowd joined in.

At the very same moment, R.B. Swaine strode through the entrance of the banquet room and stood by as he surveyed the crowd. As the clapping diminished, Swaine waltzed through the maze of round tables to make his way toward the podium.

"Go on with your remarks, Macomber," he called out from the floor. "I thought you were clapping for me," he guffawed and continued weaving his way toward his goal. His eyes fell on Karen, the only person standing.

Swaine stopped short for a brief moment, looked at her quizzically, and then walked toward his seat next to the podium.

Macomber proceeded with his remarks without acknowledging Swaine's offhand comments.

"But for those of you who are new to Clearview's Communicator's Conference, there are lots more things for you to know and do. Our job over the next three days is to keep ideas coming. Even though we continue to grow into an even more complex and technological business environment, we need to enhance our customer service. In other words, take the stuffing out of the bureaucracy.

"This means we must plan, organize, implement, and measure all of the services we currently have in place. We must also consider new ideas, as well as increase our speed, the simplicity of our operation, and the self-confidence we have in our ability to do the job. These factors," he continued, "are designed to sustain us through the rapid growth we currently enjoy and are key to any corporation's survival in the competitive environment of the twenty-first century in which we choose to flourish."

A huge burst of applause erupted throughout the banquet room.

Macomber, pleasantly surprised by the response of the group, weakly attempted to quiet the crowd with his raised hands.

"This strategy has its risks," he cautioned, "but I'm willing to bet that you guys have what it takes. You have three and a half days to work together and sort out your problems, then map out new, solid strategies for the future. I'll be anxious to hear your collective ideas at the final presentation on Wednesday afternoon. Use the time well."

The crowd stood and again applauded Macomber as he took his seat behind the dais. Without introduction, Swaine stood up and approached the microphone, pulled it further up its stem while he tapped into it, and said, "I have a few words to say to you before you begin your meal." The room suddenly fell silent.

"Macomber has a lot of faith in you as a group, and no doubt many of you have earned his admiration. But I want to go on notice by telling you that a revolution is taking place in the business community in general, and Clearview Chemicals will not remain untouched. Concepts like strategic planning, decentralization, and market research will no longer be addressed by laymen. Those jobs will be done by the experts in the field who do that kind of work night and day."

The silence was tangible. Even the waiters recognized the tension within the group and chose not to be visible while the oafish man spoke at the podium.

"I told Macomber and a dozen other people here the same thing last week." He pointed his index finger in the direction of several familiar faces in the crowd.

"In fact," he added smugly, "many of you know that I would not have approved this conference if it weren't already signed, sealed, and delivered by the time I came on board. So, my advice to you is to do what you already do, only better. Spend this time learning how to improve your own operations.

"I can't stick around here tonight because I have to go back to corporate headquarters tonight to finish up some paper work, and I'll also be in my office on Monday and Tuesday. But rest assured, I'll be here again on Wednesday afternoon to see what you've achieved, if you have achieved anything."

Macomber seethed on the side of the podium while Swaine held court. He looked downward as Swaine cut his staff to ribbons, but when he lifted his head, his eyes burned with fire.

Seconds passed as Swaine waited for some response from the audience. When none occurred, he added in a patronizing tone, "I know you're pissed off, folks, but let me put it this way: there's one thing worse than being pissed off, it's being pissed on. Do the job you're paid to do, and avoid getting caught in the drizzle."

He backed away from the podium, laughing loudly, and ambled out of the room as the assembled group watched in stunned disbelief.

Chapter Sixteen

"I told you he's going to dump all of us," said Randy Goddard to Dean after dessert. Randy, with buttons threatening to pop at any moment on his expensive fitted Brooks Brothers shirt, made little attempt to prevent this mishap, save his stained napkin that covered his bloated belly. He mentally excused his having eaten too much on the tension provoked by Swaine's vicious attack.

"It certainly sounds bad," Dean agreed, shaking his head from side to side. A member of the Michigan contingent asked Randy and Dean what had actually transpired during the few days following the New Year's break.

"It looks like there might be a bloodbath throughout the corporate departments," Randy declared with honesty. "Swaine seems to think a lot of corporate employees, particularly those of us with soft technical skills, are quite dispensable. What worries me the most is that he appears to have convinced Wainwright of that, too."

Dean responded diplomatically, "I think this could just be saber-rattling on the part of senior management to shake up whatever loose links actually exist within the departments. But if you think about it rationally, it would cost far too much money to fire and replace entire groups of people. If they're talking cost containment, it's not the way to justify a new budget."

Those who overheard Dean's comments mumbled affirmative replies.

Gunnar Williamsen, dressed in a long-sleeved flannel shirt and khakis, sat silent throughout the conversation, then added another thought. "What if Swaine's tactics are simply diversionary? Say, to cover up something else that senior management does not want employees to know?"

Everyone seated and standing around the table looked at Gunnar with bewilderment.

"Like what, Gunnar?" demanded Goddard, who had little regard for the Manager of Art Services. Williamsen was considered by most to do a second-rate job at best.

"You've all heard the stories about sick buildings on site—something the higher-ups can't seem to get a handle on. Perhaps," he said offhandedly, "they want us to worry about making a living so that the high levels of toxicity all around us seem secondary."

Dean was surprised at the absurdity of Williamsen's comments. For as far back as he could remember, Williamsen had never contributed anything of substance to any meeting they had both attended, yet he was able to meet print and visual deadlines with the precision of a well-oiled machine.

"Oh for God's sake, Gunnar," he said in a patronizing manner, "even you must know that a problem of that magnitude couldn't be covered up to that extent." Gunnar sat back, crossed his arms around his middle in his usual noncommittal manner, and did not rebuff Dean's statement.

"It could be just that Swaine's a very abrasive personality, maybe one of the most difficult ones we've encountered in our business," Dean continued.

"And he's a horse's ass," added one of the members of the group who was listening from the fringe.

Randy answered, "Maybe he'll have a fatal one-car pileup on the way back to the site and do us all a favor."

Laughter and applause burst from those gathered at the table, and a voice in the crowd called out, "I bet his wife wouldn't even arrange a funeral or even a hearse!"

*

Lydia noticed the crowd that had gathered around Dean's table. She considered joining the group to find out what they were talking about. On second thought, she decided to say goodbye to Renee and the others from Louisiana and head back.

As Lydia walked out the door of the banquet room, Gunnar Williamsen caught up to her at the coat check desk.

"Want to have a nightcap before you go back to your room?" he asked her cordially. Gunnar had never been particularly deferential to Lydia in the past, and she was mildly surprised at his offer.

"I'm kind of worn down after that performance by Swaine tonight, Gunnar. Maybe another time."

"You missed the best part," he added drolly, drawing her attention a while longer. "The people at our table were placing bets on how long he'll last with Clearview. They're actually setting odds."

"I guess there are worse ways to deal with this situation," she said politely. "How long did you decide he'd stay with the company?"

"Oh, I'm not a betting man," he countered firmly.

Lydia shrugged and said goodbye as she headed back toward Cromwell House. Behind her, she heard Gunnar greet Karen, who stopped to talk with him and accept his offer of a nightcap in the cocktail lounge. Perfect pairing, she thought with irony.

Lydia also heard Dean's laughter in the distance and sped up her pace. As she entered the Cromwell complex and headed in the direction of Room 136, she passed Christina's room and considered, for a moment, checking on her friend. She's probably fast asleep by now, she decided, and continued down the hallway, passing her own room. Lydia stopped, and doubled back.

I'll need some of my things if I stay with Dean, she thought pragmatically. I sure as hell don't want to be seen in this hallway early in the morning with these clothes on.

She opened the door of her own room, several doors away at number 124, quickly gathered her makeup, shampoo, and other accessories, plus a change of clothing for the next day, just in case. I'm no child, she assured herself, as she placed the assembled articles in the plastic laundry bag left by the hotel for its guests. Lydia carefully looked out in the hallway again. Men and women in twos and threes slowly returned to their rooms and waved goodnight to each other as Lydia entered the hallway and continued toward Room 136.

As she arrived in front of the door, she noticed the exit door at the far end of the hallway slowly closing and she heard a strange pinging sound. I wonder who would be going out at this hour, she thought.

Seeing no other activity in the hallway, she placed the key to Dean's room in the lock and let herself in. Lydia stood at the entrance of his room for a few seconds, and wondered if she had made the right decision to be there.

Indecisiveness turned into jitters as she turned away from the door with the knowledge that to stare at it would assure her that Dean would take even longer to arrive.

When the knob turned minutes later, she felt the familiar jar of internal confusion that instantly faded as he walked directly to her and drew her close.

She had wondered for months how it would feel to be held in his arms, how his skin would feel. She brushed her lips against his neck and he hugged her even more tightly.

When they finally fell apart slightly, Dean asked guardedly, "Are you nervous?" She searched his face for clues of concern for her feelings or his personal fear of discovery.

"I'm nervous about owning up to how I've felt about you for so long," she said with honesty.

"You haven't changed your mind about us, have you?" he asked as he let his arms drop with the fear that Lydia would want it that way. She answered by pressing her body tightly against his and placing her hands on his head as she kissed him deeply on his obliging mouth.

She felt his hands tremble as he pulled off her jacket and undid the buttons of her blouse, each with deliberation. He's the one who is more apprehensive about this, she thought as she anticipated the touch of his hands on her body. He slipped the blouse off her shoulders and attempted to undo her bra from behind when she subtly placed his hands on the clasp, found in the front between her breasts.

"It's been a long time since I went in search of these gismos," he laughed nervously, and she gently pushed his hands away and quickly undid the closure. Lydia stepped out of her skirt and half-slip and stood before him in her panties.

Lydia tried to undress Dean in a much more aggressive way. When the buttons on his heavily starched shirt were difficult to undo, she felt the urge to rip his shirt open with surprising strength that surged through her body.

"Hold it, hold it," he cautioned her, as he pushed her hands away from his chest, loosened his tie, opened the first two buttons on the shirt, and quickly slipped out of it. He also pulled his undershirt over his head and fired it to the floor to join the growing heap of clothing that surrounded their feet.

By this time, Lydia was deftly unbuckling his belt, and the urgency of her efforts made him double over in laughter. She moved forward, unaware as his body moved backward.

"Let's do this together," he said through his laughter. "I'll unbuckle, and you can unzip."

As he let the rest of his clothing slide to the floor, he drew Lydia close to his body by placing his hands against the base of her spine.

They stood naked, unadorned, pressed close, in an unwillingness to let space separate the depth of their feeling.

Reluctantly, he drew apart from her and led her to the bed several feet away.

"We've been friends for so long that it feels so natural to be sharing something so intimate with you," she said softly.

"Lydia, in my thoughts you've been in my arms like this so many times," he admitted openly, "that I feel as though I am picking up on what's familiar."

"I was always afraid to think of us as lovers," she replied. "I was sure that if you knew how I felt about you that you would see it in my face."

"I did," he said gently. "I knew."

Chapter Seventeen

Afterwards, they lay quietly for several moments before he reached under her head to encircle her shoulders with his arm. Lydia became aware of the cool air coming from an open window, circulating through the room. She shivered and felt a sudden wave of sadness pass through her mind, perhaps, she thought, in recognition of the unavoidable change in her relationship with Dean; perhaps in fear of what he was thinking.

Lydia wrapped her arm around Dean's chest, and he felt a stream of tears slide down the side of his body. Lydia, in her usual haste to keep order, tried to dry his body with her hand without being noticed. Dean kissed the top of her head, and said simply, "Why tears?"

"Because I'm feeling things I haven't felt for a long time, and I wasn't expecting to deal with them now." Lydia hid her face in his chest, unwilling to display the confusion and worry she was sure were evident in her eyes. Dean cupped her chin with his hand and kissed her mouth lightly.

"Lydia, you've forgotten that we've been dealing with each other's feelings for a long time now. Long before we even realized why we understood each other so well."

Lydia tried to force the unabated tears from flowing as Dean added, "I know that you're worried that making love has altered the friendship, but I think we can be even closer friends now, as well as lovers." Lydia remained silent as he continued to stroke her hair and speak.

"Don't forget, we've really been intimate friends for years without the sex. Now we can just get to enjoy what we've denied ourselves in all the time we've spent together."

He kissed her softly, and in a halting voice he said, "Would you stay with me tonight, or do you think that would be dangerous?"

Lydia was joyful, yet afraid to openly show her happiness. The fear of exposing her growing emotional attachment to Dean prevented her from shouting what feelings sprang into her head.

She was also reticent to admit that part of the time that she lay in his arms after they made love was spent considering what her bed would be like without him.

"I think we can manage it," she said with superficial calm and smiled as she thought about the clothing that lay bunched in the plastic bag next to the door.

"Do you want to talk about what Swaine said tonight?" Dean asked tentatively as he raised his back to rest against the headboard.

"I don't want Swaine to be a part of us now," she said firmly and rolled toward him so that her body pressed tightly against his. "R.B. Swaine can go fuck himself tonight."

Chapter Eighteen

The snow barreled down on the roof of Paul Frenkle's car. Frenkle thought of the people who were home having a snack in front of their fireplaces or TV's as the snow level continued to grow around the wheels of his Acura Legend. A distant lightning charge floated through the sky, and thunder roared as a microburst of stormy weather surrounded him. Anger built in larger increments as Frenkle waited to meet Cal Ferguson in the parking lot that was adjacent to Office Building One.

On this night, he was as volatile as a firecracker. He slammed the driver's side door of his Acura and kicked at the snow that grew by the inch up the rim of his tires. His annoyance at having to be at the site on a Sunday night waiting for Mr. Safety grew at the same pace. Only one other car was parked in the lot, and Frenkle knew that the Lexus belonged to Swaine.

What the hell is that shithead doing here while all his people are at the conference, Frenkle wondered. Isn't he supposed to be delivering some sort of welcoming address to the troops? I guess he just kicked ass and left for the evening, but doesn't he ever take time out to rest?

Frenkle turned to the entrance to see Cal Ferguson slowly pulling up beside him in his small red Prius hybrid. Ferguson carefully stepped out of his car onto the wet, slick pavement and tried to avoid a fall. The last thing he wanted to do was be a further source of irritation and mockery in front of his boss.

"What took you so long?" shouted Frenkle. "I've been waiting for fifteen minutes, and you are as slow as a turtle in mud."

"I couldn't help it, sir. My car is light and slips all over the road in this kind of weather. I actually left home early to be here, but a dangerous curve almost rolled me into a ditch. After that, I decided to travel even slower just so I'd get here at all."

Frenkle scoffed at his subordinate's remarks and motioned for Cal to follow in his direction.

They moved side by side but didn't speak a word. Good sense would have led them to travel arm in arm as they walked the treacherous route. Frenkle's hat already had a huge ring of snow around the brim while Ferguson's fur-rimmed coat hood deflected the storm, but they walked apart, in stark contrast to each other. Yet their responsibilities were the same: They were there, alone, to detect the source of toxicity in the air of the building.

Climbing the stairs to the side entry that led to the laboratory areas where they planned to begin their search, they shifted their feet to manage the snow building in their tracks. But despite the railings to which he held tight, Frenkle slipped and fell to his knees, barely managing not to fall on his face as well.

Cal Ferguson was right by his side to steady the man and help him rise to his feet again. Cal wrapped himself around Frenkle's waist to ensure that his boss would make it to the door without another slip.

"I guess I owe you a vote of thanks," Frenkle grudgingly offered.

"No problem," replied Cal. "I don't want us to be victims of this storm…or Swaine. We have to get this investigation done tonight, or we'll be toast."

They trudged through the white landscape to the entry, where they slid their electronic keys through the monitor. Once inside, they kicked the snow off their boots and caught the scent of a distinctly pungent smell.

"Jesus," hissed Frenkle. "Where the hell is that smell coming from?"

"Well, Sherlock," countered Ferguson, "let's follow the scent." He remarked offhandedly, as if he was enjoying the thought of the hunt.

"Don't you know how stupid you sound when you say things like that?" replied Frenkle. "You are the butt of so many jokes around here. If you weren't so good at your job, I would have gotten rid of you a long time ago, just for making me seem as foolish as you."

"You know, Paul," said Ferguson with a note of defiance, "Self-help guru Wayne Dyer says whatever other people think of me is none of my business. And I thoroughly cling to that notion."

Frenkle looked at his underling with a significant amount of admiration for the first time in their collaboration. Cal Ferguson's reason for behaving as he did finally became clear.

Step by step in the warm corridors of Office Building One, the duo worked their way over to the adjacent lab building. There they found the routine smell of used chemicals, but not the stench that permeated the entire portion of the site.

"I was sure we'd find something else in this vicinity," said Cal. "What else could provide such noxious air?"

Frenkle continued to look behind every lab table and corner, to no avail. His irritation grew as he thought of the game he was missing on TV that evening.

"Let's go downstairs in the HVAC area and check the valves and ducts," suggested Cal. "Since it's clear that there is nothing awry in the labs, it must be near the ventilation system."

As the two men turned to walk down the flight of stairs to the basement area, they moved in sequence. Cal opened doors, and Frenkle thanked him for it. Once they got to the lower level, Frenkle pointed in the direction of the vents and ducts that lead to the outdoors. The smell became more overpowering. Cal ran to the ducts and noticed that the vents were jammed. He pointed to a stinking mess of animal corpses that led to the heating system.

"Damn, it's a raccoon's nest," yelled Frenkle. "How could this be overlooked for so long?"

"It's only been a week since the odor permeated the building, Paul. By the way, can I call you Paul?

"Yeah, why not," said Frenkle as he shrugged his shoulders with indifference. "After all, you are the one who found the source of the problem."

Paul Frenkle put away his gloves and reached out to shake his safety man's hand. "You solved our problem, and you saved our jobs. I owe you a debt of thanks and a promotion."

Cal's grin creased the lower part of his face, and his heart beat faster with the satisfaction of giving his boss exactly what he needed to prove to Swaine Frenkle's worth, as well as his own.

As the two men walked up the stairway, Frenkle was mystified by what he saw as a small shadow skimming by the upper hallway and out the side door of the empty office building.

"What in hell?" he said with shock. "I swear I saw someone else in here."

"Maybe its Swaine," replied Cal. "After all, we did see his car in the lot. God only knows what he's doing here on a Sunday night. Doesn't he have something else to do besides torture the troops throughout the week?"

"Nah, the shadow was too small to be Swaine," answered Frenkle. "Do you think it was a trespasser?"

"That's another problem we can't be concerned about right now," answered Cal. "We just solved a major issue, and I don't care who was in the building besides Swaine. But if your shadow was running because of a standoff with him, I fully understand why he or she charged out of the building."

The two men crept to the entry of the hallway where Swaine's office was prominently lit. They looked through the beveled glass to see a figure behind the desk and chose to ignore the opportunity to tell him what they had found.

"Let's skip the faceoff tonight," said Frenkle. "He's the type that would want a written statement as to what was causing the problem anyhow, and this way we can have the documentation ready of what we did and how we determined the cause of the problem."

"I'll get on it first thing in the morning," said Cal. "Right after I call in the custodial department to clean out the vents and secure the entryways so that no other animals can crawl into those spaces."

In truth, Cal Ferguson felt badly for the animals who tried to escape the bitter cold and died as a result, but he kept that notion to himself. The progress he had made with his stiff, usually unwavering boss was too good to be tilted in the other direction by a careless statement of concern. He decided to keep a lot more close to the vest from then on.

<u>Chapter Nineteen</u>

Monday, January 6

Lydia lay awake in the double bed she shared with Dean as the sky outside the window turned from deep indigo to the many streaks of color created by the approaching daylight. As Dean stirred and reached for her, they watched, silently, encircled in each other's arms, as the shades changed from the deep hue to the brilliant colors of sunrise.

As the sound of the alarm they had set the night before pierced the silence, Lydia reluctantly drew away from Dean, stood up, and gathered the strewn clothing left on the floor from the night before. She shivered as she walked around the room, naked, and went to the bathroom to pull a towel from the rack to wrap around her body for warmth.

"Why modesty?" Dean said, watching her from the bed as she walked by him.

"I happen to be cold, not modest."

He reached for her again, and pulled the towel away as she crept back into the bed with him.

"You know, it's probably best that we don't sit together at any of the meetings," he said as he looked intently at her face to see her response.

"I was thinking the same thing," Lydia agreed. "It's going to be hard enough to look at you in public with any measure of indifference from now on." Dean nodded, kissed her mouth, and asked, "Does anyone, except Christina or Karen the Conference Queen, know your room number?"

Christina. Lydia hadn't thought about her friend since she passed her room the night before. She sat upright in the bed.

"Chris knows it, Dean, but she's unlikely to just stop by to see me. She'd call first or mention that she was going to come by, but after last night all bets are off."

"Let's call her," he volunteered.

Lydia nodded in affirmation, reached for her iPhone on the night table beside her, and dialed the room direct. Eight rings. There was no answer.

"What time is it?" she said to Dean as she turned to look at the clock herself to see that it was seven fifteen.

Lydia thought back over Christina's inflexible habits and realized that her friend must be walking around the grounds of the Center, just as she did early each morning in a park near her home. Lydia mentioned this habit to Dean.

"It's a good thing that she's so predictable," Dean said with a look of relief that replaced the one of uncertainty.

"I still think I better go to her room and check, just to be sure," Lydia said assertively, and she rose from the bed.

"Don't you think you ought to get dressed first?" he asked, grabbing her again and pulling her back until her head touched the pillow.

"Only if I bathe with you first."

Chapter Twenty

At seven forty-five in the morning, Dean and Lydia reluctantly left the shower when the water threatened to turn cold. Gently, Dean wrapped a large towel around Lydia's shivering shoulders and blotted the water from her body.

Lydia, enveloped in the moment, had temporarily erased thoughts of anything or anyone else from her mind. The ring of the Dean's iPhone brought her back to reality.

Without thinking, Lydia began to walk toward the phone on his night table when Dean clutched her arm and stopped her.

"My room, my phone," he reminded her quickly, and rushed for the receiver. Lydia laughed out loud then cupped her hand over her mouth as he reached the phone on the third ring.

"Yes," he said abruptly. Seconds of silence followed as Dean turned his unclad back to Lydia.

"Hi, Patti," he said passively

Lydia felt an accelerated surge of anxiety pass through her. She heard him say twice, "No, tell me now," into the phone, and she tacitly decided to return to the bathroom and close the door.

Minutes passed, and as she wondered what Dean was discussing with his wife, Lydia busied herself with the process of getting dressed.

Shortly thereafter, Dean knocked on the door. Expecting to see a look of embarrassment on his face, Lydia was unprepared for the expression of obvious devastation that was imprinted instead.

"What happened?" she asked with alarm.

Dean paused for several seconds and slowly volunteered, "She wanted to tell me a few things and hear about what's happening here."

"And so you told her everything?" Lydia said with sarcasm.

Without offering a reply, Dean walked away from the bathroom and toward the closet on the far side of the hotel room to slip on his clothing.

Still wrapped in her towel, she followed him and maneuvered her body in front of his, asking insistently, "Do you want to forget all about last night and go on with things as before? If you do, I can handle it." Her own bravado surprised even Lydia, as she stared directly up at his face.

Dean, now partially dressed, turned and pulled her to him. Markedly subdued, he lowered his head to her shoulder and held her tightly.

"You know that's not what I want," he said, finally. "I'm just embarrassed about hearing from her while we're...here."

"I know." Lydia turned her head to kiss his face, now resting on her shoulder. "Neither one of us is stupid enough to think there isn't a price to be paid for our time together."

Dean lifted his head and reached with both hands for her face. "But is the price going to end up being too stiff for you?"

"I don't know yet," she stated directly, placing her hands over his. "I guess we'll have to wait and see."

Dean kissed her hands, placed them at her sides, and reentered the bathroom to shave. In a voice that tried to replicate normalcy, he asked, "Do you think you ought to try to call Christina again?"

Lydia, pulling on a forest green wool skirt and a matching cashmere sweater from the plastic bag she had left next to the door, called out, "Good idea."

Christina's phone rang at least six times. Lydia had just removed her own phone from her ear to hang up when she heard Christina's voice.

"Where *were* you," Lydia almost shouted into the phone.

"I was just thinking the same thing about you," said an obviously offended Christina. "I called around an hour ago but you didn't answer. *Where were you?*"

Avoiding the obvious, Lydia replied, "I tried to call about the same time and when you didn't pick up, I hoped you were out doing your thing on the grounds."

"What thing are you referring to—barfing?" said Chris in a less hostile tone. Both women laughed as they referred to the prior night's incident without additional words.

"Are you feeling better?" Lydia asked with true concern.

"Better is a kind of relative thing. I'm not drunk anymore, if that's what you mean, but if you're referring to Swaine, I haven't really begun to worry yet."

"Listen," said Lydia as she slipped her feet into her shoes. "I'll pick you up at your room in a few minutes and we'll go to breakfast together. Lydia stopped and added slyly, "Unless you've already polished off another one of your prized muffins."

"There's one here for you if you want it, big mouth, but you have to treat me nice," Christina responded.

"Don't worry, Chris. I came prepared. I have my own stash of Butterscotch Krimpets down at my room."

"Well, then where are you now?" Christina asked, confused.

Lydia realized the slip of the tongue as it rolled from her mouth and casually recouped by saying, "At a courtesy phone in the hall. I went looking for a newspaper."

Good save.

"If you want to meet me in my room, you'll have to wait a few minutes longer while I change," replied Christina. "And even a little longer than that if we eat our preferred breakfast of champions before we face the others."

"You got it," said Lydia as she hung up the phone.

Lydia called out to Dean, still in the bathroom, and told him about her conversation with Chris. She also cautioned him, "Please be careful about us at the meetings."

He turned to her and asked, "Will you stay with me again tonight?"

Lydia thought about her revelation to Christina and asked, "How about staying in my room tonight instead?"

"Great," he replied, obviously relieved. "I'll stop here for my things after dinner so we can both make a clean getaway, then I'll join you in your room as soon as I can. Leave the door unlocked."

Lydia tipped her face up to give him a quick kiss goodbye, and turned away, blissful.

As she opened the door a crack, she looked up and down the empty corridor for signs of familiar faces. She walked a few steps down the hallway toward Christina's room, pausing for several seconds to marvel at the well of long-buried emotions that produced the smile wedded to her face.

Chapter Twenty One

The Christina who greeted Lydia at the door was not the woman she was used to seeing. With an ashen, slightly swollen face and red-rimmed eyes, Christina mumbled something about locating "the hair of the dog" as Lydia entered the room.

"What you need is some coffee, my dear," she said and began to pick up the phone for room service.

"Don't bother," said Christina. "There's complimentary coffee at the landings near each stairway, and the atrium downstairs has croissants and muffins if you want to get some for us while I finish getting ready."

"How did you know about that?" asked Lydia.

"They had it set up by the time I went out for my walk earlier," she replied. "My stomach wasn't ready for it when I got back, but I think I can handle it now. By the way, if they have tomato juice there too and some Tabasco sauce, will you get some of that?"

Lydia laughed wryly as she headed for the door. "As long as it doesn't have any of that dog hair you just mentioned in it," she said, and she left the room.

On the way to the hospitality table at the end of the hallway, Lydia spotted Karen Paulson talking animatedly with members of the Anaheim, California, contingent. She also could see Randy at a distance, heading toward Dean's room. As she stood in the hallway and watched, she saw Randy stop and knock. Lucky I had already left, she thought with relief, and turned again to get the coffee.

Suddenly, she felt an arm intimately encircling her waist, and half-expecting to see Dean by her side, she was surprised to find Gunnar Williamsen matching her stride as she walked. The tall, handsome blond

Swede with his angular face and broad neck was less than an inch from her face.

"Where were you last evening around ten?" he asked in a too familiar tone.

Lydia inched away from his arm and stopped to face him. "I was in my room—why do you ask?"

"I thought we could chat some more," he said suggestively, "but when you didn't answer, I assumed you made other plans."

Lydia tensed as she began to worry that perhaps he had seen her enter Dean's room.

As casually as she could muster, she answered, "I visited with some of the out-of-town people," hoping that her tightening jaw did not give her away.

Gunnar, now fully aware that his actions had inspired her to raise her defenses, backed down slightly and said, "You don't have to explain your comings and goings to me. I just wanted to spend some free time with you."

"I think not, Gunnar," she said somewhat patronizingly. "But thanks for your interest in entertaining me."

The implacable Williamsen smiled slightly, cocking his head to one side as he nodded and ambled away. Lydia suddenly became concerned about what, if anything, he actually knew about her activities of the night before.

When Lydia returned to Christina's room with the requested tomato juice, no Tabasco sauce, two mugs of coffee, and a package of Butterscotch Krimpets she had retrieved from her own room on the way, Christina had already employed the use of makeup on her sallow skin so that she appeared almost fully operative for the day.

On the floor, next to Christina's open suitcase, was a wet and muddied pair of purple satin shoes. Weren't these the shoes that Chris wore last evening? How did they get ruined—surely she hadn't worn them when she went walking out in the parking lot this morning.

The women silently ate their breakfasts of preference at the requisite round table found in every hotel room, then headed down to the main salon where a buffet awaited those who wished to eat the hearty breakfast that the conference center prepared.

"Chris, I have to ask how your purple shoes got so muddy since we put you to sleep last night. And as far as I know, you were in until your morning walk."

"Lyd, up until I saw the shoes myself this morning, I thought I had just had a bad dream in my alcoholic stupor. But apparently, what I thought was a dream was true. I must have left the side exit to the hotel and inadvertently stepped in a bed of cabbage roses that ran parallel to the building. I didn't realize that the mud created by the recent thaw stuck to my shoes as I walked toward my own car.

"I just wanted to get the cranberry-orange muffins I left in the trunk," she said simply. "Remember, I didn't eat dinner last night."

She continued to tell how she noticed a hatchback car pull into a space nearby, and how she watched a familiar figure stumble from the vehicle.

Worried that she would be seen by one of her colleagues in such a disheveled state, she told Lydia how she quickly knelt beside her car, tearing her pearls from her neck on the side view mirror.

"Don't laugh, but I honestly think I saw a clown," she explained, "because I saw what appeared to be a grotesque joker with irregular shapes of bright red blotches on the costume. And you know how I have always hated clowns."

Lydia nodded in remembrance of that fact, and said, "Go on."

"I guess I was also terrified about being seen there. Now I know that I was definitely outside and saw someone in a costume of sorts, and I hid."

Chris continued to tell Lydia how she waited several minutes after the person had entered the building, returning to her own room without the muffins. "I think I recall getting the dry heaves when I stepped onto the parking lot, and then I felt a little better. Isn't it amazing what the mind cooks up, Lyd?"

"Just keep going, Chris," said Lydia, more concerned.

"Please don't stop me if I repeat myself," she mumbled. "I'm trying to piece this thing together as best I can."

Lydia sipped her coffee and attempted to be patient as Chris continued to gesture and talk.

"I realized that I had stepped outside and didn't have my coat and was about to turn back inside when I saw the figure of someone I knew stepping out of a car. I knew that I shouldn't be seen drunk and disheveled by any of our colleagues—it could have hurt my reputation and career, so I hunched down beside the nearest car so as not to be seen by the person who was walking toward the building.

"I think that's when my pearls snagged on the side view mirror and went in all directions. The person who passed the car where I was hiding looked once in my direction when he or she heard the pearls drop, but continued to go toward the door. After the clown- like figure was gone for a few minutes, I decided to go back to my room. I got back to the hallway and realized that I didn't have my key.

"Luckily there was a chambermaid in the corridor, and I asked her to unlock my door for me. It's a miracle that I even recalled my room number. Well, she let me in and I apparently went back to sleep because that's all I can remember."

Lydia was startled by the recollection. Apparently, Chris did not dream the sequence. Perhaps Christina actually saw more than she was aware of.

"The best way to find out if you were actually dreaming or out in the parking lot is to ask the housekeeping staff if someone actually helped you reenter your room last night."

"But wouldn't that look bad for me, Lydia?"

Lydia took her friend's hand. "You must realize that the housekeeping staff remembers these kinds of movements each night. If one of the maids saw you, it's better you know about it so that you can explain, at least to yourself, what really happened. Let's go to the main desk in the lobby and see if the same housekeepers are on duty this evening."

The two threw away their garbage and left the room to head towards Converse House and up to the front desk to talk to the manager on duty, who was deeply entrenched in the local newspaper's sports pages.

Lydia took over. "I'd like to know," she asked the young man, "if the same woman who was the housekeeper for the first floor corridor of Cromwell House last evening is on duty again tonight?"

The clerk looked alarmed. "Is there a problem, ma'am?" he asked, concerned.

"No, I just need to ask her something. Is she going to be here tonight?" The clerk checked a narrow binder and ran his finger down the first page.

"Yes, it's Sonia's shift again this evening. I would guess you'd find her in that corridor or in one of the rooms from five o'clock on. I'll be sure to tell her to keep an eye out for you, ma'am."

Lydia nodded and Christina stared into space.

Relieved, the clerk wished the women a good day and returned to his paper.

"Let's find this Sonia woman tonight, Chris," said Lydia. "She'll probably be somewhere near our rooms then." They scurried across the drive and entered Cromwell House, spotting other housekeeping carts as they entered the corridor. The door to the room where the cart was parked was ajar. Lydia peeked in and saw the housekeeper turning back the sheets of the king-size bed.

"Excuse me, miss," said Lydia lightly, so as not to surprise the maid.

Sonia, the maid, walked to the doorway, and with instant recognition looked at Christina and said, "You find your key, miss?"

Christina nodded mutely as Lydia grimly watched.

"What you need today, miss?" asked the maid graciously.

"Nothing," said Christina. "Just looking in the room."

The maid said, "Ah, sí, good day, miss," and returned to her work. Lydia and Christina continued to walk down the hall in the direction of Converse House.

"Sonia must be pulling a double shift," Lydia mumbled to herself.

"It wasn't a dream, Lydia. It really happened. I was outside in the parking lot, and heaven knows where else, and I was too damned drunk to realize it." Christina placed both hands over her face and shook her head from side to side. Lydia swung her arm around her shoulder.

"Lydia, what do I do now?" she asked plaintively. "I wonder if they have anything alcoholic on the buffet..."

"You must be kidding me," said Lydia, clearly annoyed. "After last night, the thought of you and liquor should be enough to put you on the wagon for good."

"I guess you're right, but I can't relax, even though I took a tranquilizer. The ones my doctor gave me when I was going through my divorce." Chris stopped the incessant chatter and reiteration. Her eyes again filled with tears.

"When this stuff is over today, you should just kick up your feet, lie down on your bed, and watch some stupid sitcoms until they make you comatose enough to fall asleep. And if you're stupid enough to watch the eleven o'clock news, which will no doubt wake you up again, watch an old movie. I promise it will finish you off till morning."

"I wish you wouldn't use that phrase, 'finish you off.' It gives me the creeps."

"Sorry, wrong choice of words," said Lydia as she forced herself not to giggle. She took Chris by the shoulders and looked her square in the face. "Stop leaking on my sweater," she said, trying to produce a smile from the tearful woman. "You really need to calm down."

Lydia squeezed her friend again and walked to the door. "You'll be fine—I promise," she said.

Lydia looked at her watch and realized how late they had become by talking so long.

"I'm not making fun of you, but I just can't wait to figure this one out," she said as they whisked out the door. "I'd like to see this clown myself."

Lydia decided not to tell Christina about her strange exchange with Gunnar, realizing that, in the process, she'd have to expose her actual whereabouts on the night before. Although she knew full well that Christina would not pass judgment about her affair with Dean, she thought it best to keep it quiet—at least for now.

Instead, she filled her friend in on the excuse she had made for Christina's absence and described the debacle that took place at the actual dinner when Swaine made his remarks.

"I told you, Lydia, and you didn't listen to me. He's out to eliminate the entire lot of us," exclaimed Christina as they walked through the corridor.

"You could be right," Lydia nodded in agreement, "but he's doing it in such a repugnant way, I can't believe any of his recommendations would hold up to the management committee when decisions have to be made. In fact, no one expects that he's been brought in to Clearview for a stay of any duration. At least that's what everyone was saying last night.

"Chris, I'll meet you in the conference room as soon as you get yourself together. We really have to get moving."

Lydia gathered her purse and coat and hugged her friend. "You'll be okay today. We'll find out what happened to your clown later. But you want to hear the kicker?" Lydia said lightly, in an effort to improve her friend's mood, as she walked out the door. "A bunch of the guys began an actual lottery, guessing the date when Swaine will actually move on to other ventures. Now that's optimism for you."

<u>Chapter Twenty-Two</u>

Lydia entered the large conference room with Christina, and they separated to move along and talk with others whom they knew in the crowd. She found herself explaining Christina's predisposition for migraines to a group of sympathetic listeners, who were all too anxious to share their own medical histories with her.

She also felt her stomach tighten as she noticed Dean centered among a group of men and women who were involved with the political communication network within the company. Dressed in navy-colored cords and a burgundy-colored sweater that covered a light blue oxford shirt, he was relaxed among his colleagues, who were similarly dressed, and appeared not to notice as she walked by him to get a cup of coffee from the buffet table.

Karen, dressed in a simple black silk suit and a lavender blouse, looked altogether too formal for the occasion. She again positioned herself at one side of the buffet as she had at the entry the night before.

Karen checked her watch every thirty seconds, and when it approached the time she decided that everyone should assemble at the conference tables set up for work in the adjacent room, she began to shepherd small groups in that direction.

Macomber shook his head as he watched her with obvious admiration, and said to Lydia as she joined him with her coffee, "You've got to hand it to her. She's doing a really admirable job of handling this event in spite of the sour note we began with last night."

Lydia nodded in agreement. Karen was indeed doing a splendid job with the logistics. Macomber, she observed, could refer to her skill as a significant plus when he was required to detail the benefits to the company provided by the department.

"Swaine made a fool of himself," she noted reassuringly. "You never sounded better, and the contrast didn't go unrecognized by anyone."

Dan smiled at her with obvious gratitude. "That's kind of you to say, Lydia. Let's hope that Wainwright and the rest of the Management Committee see it the same way when decisions need to be made."

They walked together through the doors to the adjoining room as the first of the speakers approached the podium for the start of the first full day of the conference.

Chapter Twenty-Three

Although she did not check her watch, by 11:45 in the morning, Lydia knew it was almost noon. The empty feeling in her stomach was raging to be filled. Not entirely satiated by the package of Krimpets and the two cups of coffee she had consumed earlier, her digestive system called out for more substantial food.

Lydia was thinking about a plate of the renowned East Forge seafood pasta with avocado slices when she noticed two uniformed policemen enter the meeting room and approach Karen, who was positioned near the door.

The bewildered woman led them to Dan Macomber, and one of the patrolman whispered in his ear. A startled Macomber jumped to his feet, and with a look of shock, followed the uniformed men out of the conference room door.

The speaker continued, undeterred, but heads turned, and the participants asked one another if anyone had overheard what was said.

Before speculation could continue, Macomber grimly reentered the room followed by the police, approached the podium, and asked the speaker to step aside.

"I have some dreadful news to convey to you," he began with a voice that quavered with every word. "The Addison police were called to Clearview Chemicals today by our Site Security Force. It seems," he cleared his throat, "that Robert Swaine was found dead at his desk this morning by his assistant, Miriam Ashworth."

Those with good hearing could pick up the sound of a whispered voice in the center of the crowd triumphantly hiss out the word, "Yes." Macomber continued. "Swaine was apparently bludgeoned to death, and the police believe that the murder was committed sometime last night."

There were a few startled gasps, but Macomber, who faced the assembled group of men and women, was quick to note that there wasn't a tearful eye in the entire house.

Holy Mother, he thought. Imagine telling a group of people about the death of someone they all know, and all you can see is surprise and even delight.

Macomber continued. "There's more to tell. Miriam was the unfortunate person to discover the body. Apparently, the shock was too great for her and," Macomber paused as he saw the rapt attention of the crowd, "she was admitted to the Addison Medical Center a short while ago in shock, where she is being evaluated for a possible heart attack."

The rapt interest of the group persisted as Macomber came close to completing the most difficult part of his remarks. "The police need to question the members of the unit who work—I mean, who worked—directly with Swaine. Those of you who are part of that team, please gather in the room to my right. Since most of you have travelled a long distance to be here, we will continue with the planned agenda this afternoon."

As the shocked crowd, now talking loudly among each other, disbursed, the small group of department members who worked at the nearby site gathered wordlessly next door.

Karen turned to Lydia and said, "Why do you look so concerned? Don't you realize the murderer did us all a favor? You ought to be thrilled. Someone did us a huge act of kindness."

Lydia shrugged away her comforting arm and covered her mouth in horror. "Don't you get it," she said with unmitigated fury as she turned to face Karen. "That someone could be one of us."

Chapter Twenty-Four

Sergeant Peter Guinness was the first on the scene when the 911 call went out to the Addison police force.

"Please come and help," came the weak voice of Miriam Ashworth through the phone as she tried to remain upright while holding the receiver to her lips. By the time the first officer on the scene arrived, Miriam was beyond lightheaded, and her heart was racing like a greyhound on speed as she used her remaining strength to stay alert.

"He's dead, Officer! I'm sure he's dead!"

"Now calm down, miss. What is your name, please?"

"Miriam Ashworth, sir." With a look of terror on her face, she weakened and collapsed to the floor. Sergeant Guinness had come prepared with oxygen and first-aid equipment, as well as practiced finesse. He helped Miriam Ashworth to straighten out her body on the carpet while he quickly plugged in an oxygen tank and placed a mask to her face. Her quickened pulse was noted by the officer and written into his notebook.

Since there was no one yet in sight, he called headquarters and spoke firmly, growling into his cell phone, "Unresponsive male down. Responsive older woman down, tachycardia, on oxygen. Send a bus."

With careful dexterity, Guinness checked the pulse of Miriam Ashworth and reassured the woman that help was on the way.

With less assurance, the patrolman looked at R.B. Swaine and realized that his pale lavender-grey skin, the voluminous amount of blood that surrounded his skull and dripped to the floor, plus the lack of a pulse led to one obvious conclusion.

Once he was assured that Miriam Ashworth was more comfortable, he was able to take a better look at Swaine.

"Can you help my boss?" she called out weakly. "I don't really know if he's dead."

Carefully slipping on rubber gloves and being even more cautious where he stepped, Guinness delicately put his fingers on Swaine's carotid artery. Within seconds, he noted that the man was beyond help, and he placed a second call to headquarters to say, "Male down...DOA."

"Oh, no," cried Miriam. "I have to tell his wife," she said in an ever softer voice. Next, he noted the rigor that had developed in Swaine's body, based on his extended hand and fingers. Hours, maybe a whole day, he guessed, and he placed the information in his notepad.

As he continually checked on the condition of the fretful Miriam, who lay quietly with her feet raised by the handbag Guinness placed under them, she tried to steady her own heartbeat by repeating, "I'm alright. I'll be alright. I just need to see my doctor."

Guinness knew it would take more than a doctor's visit to stabilize the older woman and wished the ambulance would arrive soon...very soon.

Within seconds, the ambulance corps of emergency medical technicians arrived carrying a defibrillator and more sophisticated analysis equipment. The first medic slid into place and checked the pulse of Ms. Ashworth, and a second medic covered his shoes with sterile boots that prevented the man from bringing unrelated materials into a crime scene.

"Man, DOA, copious blood loss. Lividity exists, indicating that death occurred hours before discovery." The medic also wrote down that the man died from an apparent blow to the head and instantly called out to his supervisor, Sergeant Carmody, to review his findings.

"Hey Guinness," Carmody called back. "How lucky do you get to handle a crime scene of this type," he chuckled. "You got a dead guy and a sick woman."

Guinness ignored the voice and kneeled on one knee. He asked

Linda Spear

Miriam, "Is there any other way to get into this office other than the doors outside in the hall?"

"I guess," she answered. "The person who hurt Mr. Swaine could have come up any staircase with the automatic entry key we all have. He could have come in here at any time."

Good deal, thought Guinness. If someone used their automatic entry key, it would be found on the record and we'll know who did this.

"But last night," Ms. Ashworth said softly, "the safety men were here to check on the internal air quality problem we have in this building, and they could have been in here at that time. They could have even come in the side doors with their own keys."

Alarmed and concerned, Guinness called his detective in order to gather more of this information, which he realized was far beyond his own responsibility.

Cell phone at his ear, he punched in the number of his supervisor, Detective Joseph Ruschak, to further trace the trail of information that was beginning to come to light.

"Joe, there's lots more stuff coming out of this woman than her fear," he told his boss. "I think she may have answers to who was in the building when the crime occurred. You'll have to do the 'who, what, why, where and when' at the hospital where the medics are taking her."

Ruschak jumped from his desk, telling Guinness to keep the woman alert so he could interview her as soon as possible. "These things never get solved so quickly," he added. "I'd love to see it wound up today, if possible."

Minutes later, the medics who had stabilized Miriam placed her on a gurney and shuttled her off to the local hospital for further treatment.

"I just need to see my doctor," she wailed. "I'll be okay."

"Sorry Ms. Ashworth, it appears as if you've had a mild coronary event, and you'll need further tests at Community Hospital," replied Guinness cautiously.

"No, no," she screamed. "I want to go home. I want to put all of this away and sleep in my own bed!"

The medics discounted the woman's pleas and gently placed her on the gurney before taking her down the nearby stairs to the ambulance for the five minute trip to the local medical center. The police could hear her cries all the way down the stairs. "I want to go home! I want to go home!"

Linda Spear

Chapter Twenty-Five

The forensic team and crime scene officers, led by Detective Joseph Ruschak, began their examination of Swaine's office by videotaping the crime scene.

The body was first checked by alternating light sources and luminol, a colorless chemical fluid, to distinguish fibers, finger prints, tracks of blood, and other fluids. On Swaine's jacket, the police recognized fibers that did not coincide with his other clothing; and the floor, examined in the same way, indicated boot marks of a man or woman with small feet—perhaps even Ms. Ashworth's own shoe print.

Ruschak called out to Guinness and Sergeant Carmody. "I'm certain we have some vital evidence on the body and the floor. We have to get this stuff collected now before the coroner's truck comes for pickup."

The men worked diligently to bag and label every possible specimen and place them in collection envelopes for the ME's group to identify.

Within the hour, the medical examiner's team bagged Swaine and placed him in the coroner's truck to be taken to the medical examiner's office for the post-mortem to begin.

Chapter Twenty-Six

Seated around a long conference table in the Converse Center, the members of the corporate relations group from the nearby site ate lunch in silence. Accompanying them at the table were Detective Joseph Ruschak of the Addison Police Department and his assistant, Sergeant Peter Guinness.

Christina stared dejectedly at her uneaten tuna fish salad, and the others, Dean, Randy, Gunnar, Dan, Karen and Lydia, as well as the two policemen, ate heartily from piled high plates that they had filled at the buffet table.

Lydia, afraid to look directly at Dean, could imagine the conversation and celebration they'd have over Swaine's bad fortune later on in her room.

As she sat amidst the confusion about her role at Clearview Chemicals, she thought of how she loved the chance to mold the external image of the company and now would be the best opportunity.

How many times, she thought, does a person have to explain toxic waste, ocean dumping, and non-biodegradable materials produced by our company to the public? Too many times, she admitted.

On the other hand, as a consumer, her cynical view of what was being done to the environment and the land the company worked on was something she knew how to keep to herself.

Snapped out of her reverie, Lydia heard Detective Ruschak say, "This food is as good as they say it is," through a mouth half-filled with shrimp salad. "I'm glad we decided to have a bite before we get down to business." Sergeant Guinness sat by, taking a large swig from his cup of coffee.

Ruschak finished his meal, stood, and began.

"Let me begin by saying that under no circumstances have we begun to identify suspects at this time. But, from what we've been able to piece together so very early in the investigation, we think the crime was committed by someone familiar with the site. So," he said as he took a sip of water, "in order to get a sense of what may or may not have happened in the Corporate Relations Department in your absence, we need to talk with you together and individually about Mr. Swaine."

Ruschak furtively observed those assembled in the conference room. He was quick to note carefully practiced indifference displayed by this small group of men and women—all except for the woman named Christina. He had the advantage of knowing their names because all the conference participants were required to wear nametags. This skinny blond broad, he thought to himself, looks like she lost a lot more than just a boss in this mess. I bet there is more information to be gained from her than the others, if I go after it right now.

He pointed in Christina's direction and said, "Miss, could you please give me your name and position at Clearview Chemicals?"

Christina gave an involuntary shudder, and she pushed herself away from the table with her hands. Slowly, as she often did under duress, she began to thread her fingers through her hair.

"My name is Christina Benderhoff. I work for Karen Paulson in the internal communications section of our department." She nodded in Karen's direction, who, seated across the table, looked up momentarily, smiled, then concentrated on peeling an orange.

"Ms. Benderhoff," continued Ruschak as he rose from his chair and moved closer to the disheveled woman, "could you tell me how well you knew Mr. Swaine, and how you would characterize your relationship with him?"

Christina twisted the engagement ring she continued to wear on her right hand over and back on her knuckle, and she kept her head bowed as she appeared to be concentrating on recall.

The Iceman Checks Out

"Relationship," she mumbled. "I hardly knew the man. He just joined the company last week, and we hadn't really worked with him as a group yet."

"But had you dealt with him directly since his arrival, or, perhaps..." He paused. "Did you know Mr. Swaine before he began to work for your company?"

Christina looked directly into Detective Ruschak's face and replied angrily, "I know what you're implying officer, but you're way off base. The truth is he wasn't happy with what he had seen of my work. In fact, he told me that I had wasted my time and the company's money on something I worked on for the latter part of last year. But I didn't have anything to do with his murder," she said intensely, her eyes filling rapidly with tears. "I'm upset because..."

"Because, why, Ms. Benderhoff?"

"Because my fingerprints, and probably those of some of the others here are going to be found in his office. I was in there on Friday afternoon when he told me that he was thinking of hiring a top-notch communications consultant to redo my work on the annual report." Christina continued to wind the ring around her finger until it accidently slipped off and fell from her hands.

Guinness, who was leaning against the far wall with his arms and legs crossed, followed the ring as it bounced on the rug and bent to retrieve it as Christina lunged for it herself.

A resounding crack could be heard as their heads met on the way. Christina put her hand to her head, sat directly on the rug with her legs akimbo and began to sob once more. Sergeant Guinness, with one hand on his own head, reached carefully under her arm with his hand to help her to her seat.

"I'm sorry," she wailed. "God, what am I apologizing for?"

Detective Ruschak looked at her curiously.

"You probably think that I killed him because I'm so upset." She lifted her head and tears streamed uncontrollably down her cheeks. "I still have the remnants of a bad headache I developed last night, and I don't feel very well, especially after hitting my head against that policeman."

Lydia rose quickly and handed her a wad of bunched up napkins to mop her wet face.

"Tell me about last evening, Ms. Benderhoff," Ruschak asked gently. Lydia watched him carefully, afraid that Christina would tell how she spent the evening in bed, instead of in plain sight with her colleagues. She looked across the table at Macomber, who appeared quite agitated as he chewed frantically on a thick white straw.

Christina looked directly at Lydia seated to her left and across from Dean, and then to her right at the head of the table where Ruschak stood patiently.

"I was drunk and got sick," she whispered as her head lowered slowly to her chest.

"Just when and where did this happen?" Ruschak asked quickly, not wanting to let this bit of information get lost.

"It all started around six o'clock in the conference center bar. I went there to meet some friends before the dinner—to loosen up," she said methodically, as if to make sure that everything was explained as carefully as she could manage.

"But I didn't have anything to eat, except a few pretzels, and the liquor went straight to my head—and my stomach." Christina turned to face Lydia.

The others surrounding her at the table looked at Christina with empathy, as well as a few snickers.

"Thank God Lydia was with me. Actually, she tried to slow me down, but I wouldn't listen. So when it came time to go to the dinner in the banquet hall upstairs, I could barely move. I could feel the booze swimming in my head and my stomach. So Lydia helped me to my room. Actually, I think Dean helped me, too. They got me into my bed, after I threw up, actually, and I think I passed out."

Ruschak looked at Lydia and asked, "Is all of what Ms. Benderhoff said true?"

Lydia nodded in agreement. "I tried to stop her from drinking so much, but she was intent on getting buzzed. I don't believe that she had any idea of how much she actually put away. I think it was about four martinis."

"Whew," Ruschak whistled appreciatively. "That would lay me flat too with no food in my belly," he added.

Christina started to cry again.

"When you brought her back to her room, did you help her to undress and get into her bed?"

"I helped her brush her teeth after she threw up," volunteered Lydia, "but I didn't attempt to take off her clothing. Dean was with me," she nodded in his direction, "and we just managed to get her shoes off and cover her up in bed. We also left her light on and her room key next to her travel alarm clock."

"Why did you leave a light on, Ms..." Ruschak looked closely at Lydia's name tag and said, "Ms. Barrett and..." he looked in Dean's direction.

"Handlesman," said Dean.

"Mr. Handlesman."

Dean said, "We talked about it and thought it best to leave a light on for her, just in case she needed to make a quick trip to the bathroom again."

There was a ripple of nervous laughter around the table from everyone except Christina, who sat erect with a continuous stream of tears rolling down her face.

"So when you left her at around—what time, Ms. Barrett?"

"Around seven o'clock, I think. We had to get to the dinner. I remember telling Chris that I would make excuses for her not being there because she, even in that state, was concerned about what people would say if she wasn't there, and she was right."

"What did you say about her absence?"

"I told anyone who asked that Chris had a migraine headache, but actually very few people noticed that she wasn't there. They were taken up with their own interests. That's the way it usually is," she stated flatly, and most of those in attendance nodded in agreement.

"Did you check on her again last night, after the banquet?" Ruschak asked Lydia, and he looked as well in Dean's direction. Lydia began to speak first.

"Actually, I passed her room on the way to my own, and I thought about checking on her. But I really didn't want to disturb her sleep, so I went on ahead."

"What about you, Mr. Handlesman?"

"I thought about it too," he said, "but I didn't want to disturb her either. Frankly, I was afraid that if I woke her up, she'd be even sicker. You know how that can happen if you haven't slept off the alcohol before you get up." More nervous laughter arose from the group.

"So we have no assurance that you stayed in your room all night, Ms. Benderhoff." He stared directly at a disquieted Christina.

"How could I do anything else?" she replied shrilly. "I was shitfaced drunk and was lucky that my friends got me back to my room before I puked and passed out in front of everybody."

A roar of involuntary laughter was met with Christina's sobs. Lydia's heart ached for her friend, but she struggled to keep her face impassive.

Who's next, she thought.

Christina rose, looked at the detective, and said, "I have to use the restroom. Please let me out of here."

Ruschak bowed his head, knowing that his incessant pounding on Christina had long passed the polite interview stage of interrogation. He nodded in the bereft woman's direction as she ran from the room. Her tears escalated with every step and could be heard far down the hallway.

Quiet permeated the room, and even the sounds of the kitchen workers next door who were cleaning up the lunch buffet could not be clearly detected.

"Let's just go around the table and let me get names and a sense of who you are." Ruschak's eyes rested on Randy, who sat next to Lydia at the table.

"I'm Randall Goddard, sir. Randy for short. I'm the issues management man at Clearview Chemicals." Randy leaned back in his chair, trying to appear nonchalant. He didn't notice that the buttons of his shirt barely closed across his midriff and strained precariously against the cotton fabric as he attempted to appear casual.

"Just what does an 'issues management man' do, Mr. Goddard?" Ruschak said with a less than subtle hint of sarcasm.

Randy, perplexed by his need to discuss himself at all with the police, appeared not to notice.

"It means that when the company faces issues involved with its production or business orientation that have an external public at odds with these practices, I monitor the situation and make recommendations to the company as to what to do."

"What, for instance, are some current issues?" asked Ruschak, now appearing to be fairly interested.

"Animal testing, for one," replied Randy, now less nervous as he discussed his own field. "Environmental pollution for another, and waste minimization. That's a big one."

"How did you and Mr. Swaine see your responsibilities?"

"Actually, we hadn't gotten into much of a discussion." Randy appeared to tighten up again. "But then again, I don't think he fully understood the value of my job."

"Why do you say that, Mr. Goddard?" Ruschak said as he jotted down a note on a small tablet he had placed on the table.

Randy straightened up a bit in his chair as he self-consciously pulled the front plackets of his shirt together and said, "Swaine didn't know how much responsibility is required of my job. He thought that it could be done by somebody with a lesser title, who they could pay less money."

Randy became more agitated. "He didn't realize that activist groups don't respect a company that doesn't pay heed to these issues, and by assigning a peripheral player to that job they are telling the public that the issues don't matter much to the company. So that's what I was doing last night after the banquet, talking with my counterparts from the other company sites. We were all at the bar until way past midnight."

"Goddard's right," interjected Macomber. "The last thing Clearview Chemicals needs now is for the local public to think that we don't have a shared concern about our environment. I've heard that Swaine had a habit throughout his entire career of simply looking at the bottom line."

"You appear to know quite a bit about Swaine's business performance, Mr. Macomber. Could you tell us more about him and how you and he began your mutual relationship?"

"Do either of you have a cigar handy?" Macomber ripped the straw out of his mouth and looked frantically around the table.

Ruschak barely smiled and said, "I'm sorry, but I don't smoke, sir."

"Shit." Macomber grabbed a new straw and jabbed it into his mouth. Guinness volunteered, "If you want me to check with the catering staff, I'll run over and see if they have any cigars, sir."

Karen, who was seated next to Macomber at the other end of the table, placed her hand over the hand of her boss and told Guinness, "That won't be necessary, Sergeant. Mr. Macomber has just recently given up smoking. I think he's just reacting to the stress of this situation."

"I'll speak for myself, Karen," growled Macomber and pulled his hand away. "It's alright, Sergeant. She's right, but thanks for trying to help."

Macomber held firmly to the straw, now clenched tightly between his teeth.

"And your relationship with Mr. Swaine, sir?" asked Ruschak for a second time.

"You can't call it a relationship," muttered Macomber. "If you really want the truth, it was more like cold war. The guy was a horse's ass, and everyone who knew him will tell you that. It doesn't take months, or even weeks, to understand his type. The guy had no soul. All you had to do was look into his eyes. Scary stuff. He was just like Randy said, a numbers man; someone who was only interested in the bottom line, and that made it all the more difficult for people like us. We're service oriented," he continued, sounding more and more like the Macomber that his department members knew well.

"Swaine wanted this group to work like robots, at minimal expense and maximum speed, without concern for any of us as individuals. You can't do that in our business. You have to recognize the customer, be it the media, other employees, the environmentalists, the politicians, and even senior management, as worthy of time and attention. How else can you communicate with so many unless you make an effort to direct your message to each one as if they are your only client?"

Macomber sank back down into his seat, satisfied that he had made his point clear.

"Then why was he brought into your operation, Mr. Macomber, if everything was proceeding as well as you believe it to be?"

Macomber leaned forward again, this time placing both elbows on the table. "It has everything to do with the economy, Detective Ruschak. "Please don't think I don't consider number crunching important at all. If we didn't look at the numbers, we'd be delinquent in our responsibility to the company. What I'm saying is there are more reasonable ways to cut costs other than what he projected, but Swaine was more than willing and quite able to cut a wide swath across our budget, slicing out pieces that we know to be vital to our operation, and he wasn't willing to listen to reason. We all knew that, and we all feared what it might mean to our department and to each of us as individuals."

Ruschak was impressed with Macomber's assessment of Swaine and kept it in mind with what others had preliminarily told him about the man.

"Was your job threatened by his arrival?" he asked the department head.

"I have to tell it to you straight, Detective. I plan to retire in about five years, but the more I got to know about that jackass, I began to consider retiring at the end of this year. Maybe," Macomber declared, "he wanted me out of here sooner than that, but if you think that's a reason to kill him, you're very much mistaken. I disliked the man, hated him for that matter, but not enough to want to kill him."

"I understand you, Mr. Macomber. I don't think anyone hated him enough to want him killed except the person who murdered him, and that's why I have to spend this time finding out more about the man and who could have cared enough to go to that extreme.

"Can you think of anyone who could have been in contact with him at the site last evening? In other words, do you know if anyone was at the corporate site around the same time?"

Macomber looked at his employees. Each one—Lydia, Randy, Dean, Karen, and Gunnar—stared at him with varying degrees of concern. "If you're asking where I was during that period of time, I know I was with Randy in the bar. Just ask him. We all needed to unwind after the brainless remarks that Swaine made at the banquet. Just ask anyone here how demoralizing his comments were to the entire group of us.

"As far as these people are concerned, I know that none of them were over at the site at any time yesterday, but I think you might want to contact the Site Director, Paul Frenkle, and his Safety Manager, Cal Ferguson. They planned to do some testing on our ventilation system during the day yesterday, and although I don't think they were there last night, they might be able to give you some answers."

"Thank you, Mr. Macomber." Ruschak wrote down the names of the two men Macomber suggested and then directed his gaze to Gunnar Williamsen, seated on his right.

Gunnar, aware that he was next to be questioned, announced proudly, "I am Gunnar Williamsen, the manager of Art Services, and I produce the creative aspects of the printed material that my colleagues seated here with me write."

The detective noted the various mix of annoyance and ridicule displayed on the faces of the others seated at the table. It was clearly evident that Williamsen was not well respected among his colleagues.

"Tell me, Mr. Williamsen, what was your relationship with the deceased?"

Gunnar picked up one of his hands from the table and examined his nails before he spoke. "I had no relationship with the deceased, Detective Ruschak."

"Well then, how well did you know the deceased, Mr. Swaine?"

Williamsen smiled broadly, showing even, white teeth. "Know him? I hardly even talked with the man," he stated bluntly and waited for more.

"Let me put it to you more clearly, then. Had you met with Swaine at any time during the short period that he oversaw your operation, and what kind of relationship had you established?"

Gunnar Williamsen pushed himself away from the table and slung one leg over the other knee. "I really didn't care what kind of relationship we did or didn't have, Detective Ruschak. You see, my job is safe. My sister is married to the CEO of the company, Charles Wainwright. That makes Wainwright my brother-in-law. His children are my nieces and nephews. Do you think I gave a damn what Swaine thought of me?"

Williamsen slapped his hand on the table and aggressively stated, "Truthfully, Detective, Swaine said my work was mediocre at best, but you know what? He said that about most of these people seated here, whether it was true or not. They may have taken him at his word, but I didn't. I don't give a shit what he thought of me. I wonder if he told that to my brother-in-law, but I bet I know what kind of reaction he received."

Macomber retorted, "How kind of you to be so concerned about your fellow workers, Williamsen. At this point, it doesn't matter what he thought of your work, does it?"

Gunnar smiled broadly at Macomber. "Point well taken, Daniel. I take that back. I don't give a shit what he thought of me. Now it matters even less." Gunnar chuckled to himself and continued to examine his hands.

Ruschak watched the tension mount between Macomber and his art manager. Something I ought to keep an eye on, he thought to himself, and he made a note of the same in his notepad. He then centered his gaze on Karen Paulson, who had just finished eating her orange. Walking toward her, she turned to face him and smiled warmly.

"Your name is Karen Paulson, I see. And your title, miss?"

"I'm the Internal Communications Manager at the site, sir. I see to it that employees are informed about all events, Human Resource benefits, and situations relevant to their work at Clearview Chemicals," she said proudly. "In fact, I'm wholly responsible for this communicator's conference, sir. I'd be glad to tell you more, but I don't think I should take up all of your time."

Ruschak was impressed with the style of this woman. Not only was her softly highlighted, shoulder-length blond hair and muted makeup perfectly done, but he observed something he personally valued. Her shoes appeared to be highly polished, like the businessmen who work to maintain their appearance out in the trade.

Her suit, he noticed, was well pressed, and although the others were dressed more casually as they apparently had been told to do, Karen Paulson was dressed for business and business alone. She's a good looking woman, he thought approvingly. I bet Swaine didn't have any problem with her.

"Ms. Paulson, I'm afraid I have to ask you the same questions as everyone else," he said almost apologetically. Lydia looked across the table at Dean. Karen's pulling off her usual male-ego-flattery act on this poor schnook, she conveyed through eye contact.

"Go ahead and shoot, Detective," Karen said happily. "Oh, I don't mean that literally," she added, laughing heartily—and alone.

"Don't worry, Ms. Paulson. Swaine wasn't killed with a gun. He was hit with a blunt object."

"Either way," she laughed nervously, "he ended up dead, didn't he?"

"Where were you last evening between the hours of eight and midnight?"

Karen turned to Gunnar, tapped his knee, and said lightly, "Having a drink with this gentleman, sir."

Gunnar smiled broadly at Karen. He turned back to Ruschak and said, "This is true, Detective. After the dinner, I spoke briefly with Ms. Barrett seated over, but she was in a big hurry to return to her room. I then asked Ms. Paulson to join me for a nightcap in the bar. She and I spent an hour or two together before we...retired for the evening."

"What do you mean 'retire,' Williamsen?" said Ruschak, showing obvious displeasure at the manner in which Williamsen was addressing his line of questioning.

"Oh, don't get me wrong, Detective," Williamsen said with a chuckle. "I didn't retire for the night with Ms. Paulson, but by the time we both went to our respective rooms, it was late and time to go to sleep."

"Around what time was that?" repeated Ruschak, obviously running out of patience.

"Between eight and ten, I expect. Karen said she had some calls to make from her room about tomorrow's schedule, and I saw her back to her door."

"That's true, Detective. I got back to my room around ten and called the facilitators for today's presentations to see if there were any loose ends to clear up beforehand."

"Were there?"

"Were there what?" Karen asked brightly.

"Any loose ends." Ruschak began to have second thoughts about Karen Paulson. Was she playing him, or was this the manner in which she always answered questions?

"No loose ends, Detective. I went to bed relaxed and ready to deal with today's schedule. It's amazing how much things can change in twelve hours."

"You could say that again," mumbled Dean, seated next to her.

"Mr. Handlesman, we haven't heard much from you so far. Could you please offer us your share of this conversation?"

Dean looked directly at the detective and said, "I guess I ought to start by saying that I hardly knew anything about Swaine. In fact, except for the joint meetings, I was fortunate enough not to have had contact with him. I say fortunate because everyone else who met with him prior to the conference last week was scared stiff about their jobs. I just hadn't had my chance to get personally shaken up yet."

"And your job at the company?" asked Ruschak as he wrote furiously in his notepad.

"I am what you'd call a lobbyist. I am the person that the company sends out to talk with the politicians about pending legislation. It's my job to help influence them to vote on bills that work in favor of our corporation and the industry in general."

"And are you successful in your job?"

Dean noted that this was the first time that Ruschak had asked this question of anyone. He thought to himself that it must be because he was the only one so far who had not been personally attacked by Swaine prior to his death.

"I'd say so," said Dean modestly. "It's a win one day, lose another day proposition. This is not an easy era to try to influence legislators. Their constituents are quite well informed and very vocal as to how they choose to vote. We are dealing with an intelligent public."

"I know what you mean," Guinness interjected. "My wife is an animal activist. She gets real upset when she talks about product testing done on animals by chemical companies. She's one of the people who tried to get people like you to develop computers capable of simulating your results. I won't even tell her who I met with today. She'd have my ear, asking if you guys are involved with the testing."

Guinness looked more carefully at Dean and said, "What did you say your name was again?"

"Handlesman. Dean Handlesman."

"You know, I think I went to your wedding a while back." He stared more intently. "Yes, I know I did. You married my cousin Patti Reardon, didn't you?"

Dean looked utterly surprised as he was forced to answer yes. He had married Patti Reardon almost three years ago and had little recollection of the assorted group of his wife's relatives who assembled at the church that day.

"Yes, I remember you. She was so happy, you know? I haven't seen her since then. The family is not that close you know, but send her my best will you?"

"And what's your first name, Officer?" Dean asked automatically.

"Peter. I'm her first cousin on her mother's side." Sergeant Guinness added coyly, "Got any kids started yet?"

"Not yet." Dean could sense Lydia's discomfort and made careful effort not to look in her direction.

"Sorry to interrupt family business between you two," said Ruschak, abruptly, "but I need to know what you were doing last evening."

"After dinner, I went back to my room," Dean explained. "You heard about Swaine's diatribe at the podium. None of us was in a partying mood after that."

"Can anyone attest to your whereabouts, Mr. Handlesman?"

Dean kept his eyes affixed on the detective, but he knew he sensed Lydia's tension.

"Sorry, but I think you'll have to take my word for it."

Ruschak continued to make notes and turned lastly to Lydia. "And last, but not least, Ms. Barrett."

"I'm the External Communications Manager, but I want to know before we start if you could find out if the media has gotten wind of Swaine's death yet?"

"If they have noticed the police activity at your site, the answer is yes, but I doubt if the police blotter has recorded the information yet. Is that a problem for you?"

Lydia shifted in her seat, uncomfortable with the responsibility she knew would shortly be hers.

"When they call the company for answers, it's me they need to speak to. I think I should find out if there have been any inquiries yet."

Ruschak nodded in agreement and turned to his assistant. "Yo, Guinness. Call headquarters and find out how much the media knows about the case so far. We have the company flack in here, and she wants to do her job."

Lydia looked down the table at the others. She saw Dean mouth the word "flack" and start to laugh. Karen played with a piece of her orange skin, and Lydia heard Randy stifle a burp.

Ruschak turned again in Lydia's direction. "You want to tell me about Swaine, Ms. Barrett?" he asked patronizingly.

"There's precious little to tell, Detective. He was with us for so short an amount of time that we really didn't get to know much about him."

Linda Spear

"According to what Ms. Ben..." He stopped to check his notes for the correct pronunciation of Christina's name and began again. "According to what Ms. Benderhoff and the rest of you have said in front of all of us, Swaine started out on the wrong foot with all of you, and that contributed to his death. Is that true?"

Lydia had already prepared her response as she saw where he was leading. "Swaine had a built in reputation in the industry as a hatchet man. We didn't have any illusions about what he was brought in to do at Clearview. What we didn't know until last week was to what extent he would reduce our workload or our responsibilities in the company. To be perfectly honest, Officer, if I may speak for everyone here, we were planning to keep our distance from Mr. Swaine and hope for the best. No one here, I fully believe, had any reason to want him dead."

Ruschak looked at the others and said, "Do you all agree with Ms. Barrett's statement?"

Karen and Randy nodded, and Gunnar volunteered, "Lydia's right in saying that Swaine posed a potential threat to our day-to-day operations and our budgets, but I can't agree that we all feared that he'd cause us to lose our jobs or do any real harm."

Gunnar sat back in his chair, looking very smug to everyone, including Detective Ruschak.

"Do you agree, however," the detective said pointedly, "that Ms. Barrett's statement about Swaine's threat to certain people's jobs could have caused his murder?"

Lydia interjected, "I didn't say anything of the sort, Detective. I only said that no one here, just as Dan said before, could have cared enough to want him dead. Am I right?" she asked of the group as she looked from face to face.

There were muffled responses of "right" and "of course."

Lydia noticed Guinness approaching the door. As she looked in his direction, Detective Ruschak turned and asked, "What's the status with the media?"

"It's a good thing you asked me to check on it, Joe. The local papers and some of the news services are lined up at the company's main entrance, and they keep on calling police headquarters from their phones for information."

Lydia got up from the table. "I really should head back to the site, Detective. Am I free to go?"

Karen Paulson stood as well, saying, "It's my job to inform the other employees, Detective Ruschak, and I'd like to be allowed to go back to the site now."

Ruschak nodded abstractly in her direction and pointed his pen at Lydia.

Karen pushed her purse under her arm and quickly walked away from the assembled group. Her heels clicked in rhythm on the banquet room floor as she turned the corner and headed for Cromwell House.

"Before all of you decide it's time to leave, I have one last question of Ms. Barrett over here. Can you account for your whereabouts last evening?"

Lydia stood, ready to make a clean breakaway, and replied, "I went back to my room, took a long hot shower, and went straight to bed." She thought, that was pretty close to the truth as long as he doesn't ask me if I was alone.

"Did you speak with anyone else that evening?" Now here was the hard part.

"Sorry, Detective, wish I could be more helpful, but I really need to get back to the corporate site."

Gunnar interrupted their dialogue. "I knocked on your door around ten, Lydia," he said slowly, "after I left Karen. I thought you might want to continue our conversation."

Lydia was not prepared. She knew quite well that by ten she was in Dean's room, lying in his arms.

"That must have been when I was in the shower," she replied without missing a beat. "Now, if I can leave, Detective Ruschak?"

Ruschak noticed the petite, delicate frame that encompassed this quick-thinking, dark-haired woman with magnificent cheekbones and huge brown eyes. He thought to himself that, under other circumstances, she'd be worth getting to know.

"Do you have a car here, or do you need a ride back to the site?"

"I have my own car," she said and turned to leave.

"I'll need to talk with you more, Ms. Barrett," Ruschak called out to Lydia. "Stick around your office, and don't leave till I catch up with you again."

Lydia looked back in his direction and noticed Dean's alarmed expression. "Don't worry," she called out. Ruschak thought she was speaking to him.

As Lydia left the room, Ruschak turned to the others still seated, backs to the table.

"Macomber, what do you think? Should your group remain here with the others at this conference, or do you want them back at their desks during the investigation?"

Macomber made brief eye contact with his employees and recognized their desire to return to the site, if for no other reason than to learn more about what had happened there the night before.

"I think they'd like to keep their own operations in hand, Detective.

If you agree, I think we should all return to our desks, and that way we can be available to meet with you as you see fit."

Ruschak nodded vigorously as Macomber talked. He wanted to have access to the people who he deemed most anxious to see the dead man out of the way.

"But I'd like to keep you all together in the evening," Ruschak called out as they scuttled to the doors. "So don't get completely caught up with your jobs. Plan to return to the conference center at the end of the work day." With a subtle wave of his hand he summarily dismissed the rest of the group, which quickly disbursed in every direction.

Lydia walked down the hall to exit the conference center main building, looking in every direction to locate Christina, but she was nowhere in sight.

Where the hell did that woman go?

<u>Chapter Twenty-Seven</u>

Before heading back to the site to develop and dispense accurate information for the media and other employees, Lydia ran directly to Cromwell House to Christina's room to see if her friend was even more upset over the cross examination she had endured from Ruschak.

What did he glean from his conversation with her and the others? What did Randy reveal about the way the company handled animal rights protestors? What did Dean do to persuade politicos to support the chemical industry? And what in hell could Karen tell him about all the employees' responsibilities with which she was so involved?

Or was he looking for guilt in anyone's eyes?

Poor Christina. That fall from grace put her on her duff and, as usual, had her crying her eyes out.

Lydia shook her head in disgust as she knocked on the door in a way that Christina would recognize as her friend's calling card. That would surely draw the distraught woman out of her bed where she pictured Chris to be. Lydia was certain that's where she would find her friend in tears.

Yet there was no answer.

More insistent knocking did nothing to bring her friend to the door. As one of the chambermaids rolled her cart by the door, Lydia casually asked, "Could you let me into my room? I seem to have forgotten my key."

Without question, the pleasant cleaning woman pulled out her master key and easily slipped it into Christina's locked door.

"Thanks so much," Lydia said with true gratitude. The woman would never know it wasn't her own room she helped her enter.

Once inside, Lydia looked straight at the bed tossed with sheets and blankets that she thought with amusement could have indicated quite a night of sexual healing, if she had gotten so lucky.

But Christina was not in the bed. And, as Lydia scoured the room for signs of her friend, her pulse raced. Was it her imagination, or did she see blood coming from the floor of the bathroom? Were there drops and blotches along the carpet that led to the closet set into the wall next to the door?

Lydia felt fear that she didn't want to handle by herself, but since there were no people around to search for Christina with her, she gathered her wits and headed for the closet.

Slowly, with hands shaking uncontrollably, she opened the creaking door and witnessed a scene she had only observed on TV and in movies. There was her friend, her body balled up in a corner of the closet, bloodied from head to toe and looking like a broken marionette whose strings had just been cut.

As Lydia fell to her knees to reach for her friend, she noticed that the open vacant eyes ensured that Christina Benderhoff was indeed a dead duck.

Chapter Twenty-Eight

Lydia heard screams, loud and shrill, bouncing off walls, yet they came from nowhere specific. How long would it take for her to realize that the shrieks stemmed from her own lungs?

Her hands felt sticky, and she looked to see blood dripping from her fingers and her elbows. Kneeling next to Christina's body, her bloodied knees were warm and tacky as well.

Lydia had become almost as blood-covered as the newly minted corpse that had once been Christina.

Lydia couldn't bear to stare too long at the sight of her friend. There was something so pathetic about this already vulnerable woman in her state of death.

Lydia turned away from the spectacle as if she could will it away. Could Chris have crawled into the closet by herself to get away from the insistent blows that must have rained down on her?

Or, could Chris still be alive? Even Lydia knew all too well that the dull, sightless eyes explained her disappearance of her spirit.

"Chris, Chris, oh Chris," she whimpered as her voice became louder and louder.

Lydia's body felt shaky and weak as she tried to rise to a standing position, but her head began to spin just as footsteps approached.

Could they be the feet of Christina's killer? Without a thought left in her mind, her legs gave out and she collapsed to the carpet, hitting her head with a thud.

Chapter Twenty-Nine

Moments later, a housekeeper ran into the room to seek out the source of the screaming and discovered Lydia semiconscious on the floor. Without looking for the source of Lydia's frenzy, the hysterical cleaning woman darted from the room and in a thick foreign accent, she yelled "MURDER, BLOODY MURDER," up and down the hallways.

Lydia rose slowly when she heard the woman's voice pulsating through the halls at a short distance. With all the effort she could muster, she hoisted her body up on her hand and knees and waited to be found alongside Chris' body. Her heart was beating so fast that she found taking gulps of air very difficult to do.

I won't scream any more, she thought to herself. I'll wait until someone comes to help me deal with this.

Thoughts of Dean rattled through her brain as she wondered if he had left for the site yet or if he was still in the conference center and able to assist her. His name was poised on her lips, but she began to grind her teeth in order not to be heard calling his name.

Thundering noise intensified in the hallway, and Lydia knew that people were on their way to see the desperate site.

How can I explain what I'm doing here, she thought to herself as Ruschak ran in to gape at her and the body. Lydia noticed that he put latex gloves on his hands.

"What the hell happened here?"

Lydia stared up at Detective Ruschak and shook her head in despair.

"I found her here," she whispered. "I found her like this," she mumbled and pointed at Christina's crumpled body.

Linda Spear

Ruschak took over. "I'll help you to stand up, Ms. Barrett," he said perfunctorily. "I'll need to talk with you outside the perimeter of the crime scene and examine your hands and clothing. Did you touch the body or anything else?"

Lydia felt like a pillar of stone. She could not move or speak. Time seemed non-existent, as if she was on autopilot. Without thought, she put out her hands to be examined.

Will he handcuff me, she thought to herself, wishing she could rub the back of her throbbing head, which had hit the floor with force.

As if he read her mind, he said, "No handcuffs, Ms. Barrett. You have your hands pointed at me as if I was going to slip them on you. Do you have a reason for that?"

"Hell, no," shouted Lydia who finally found her voice. "I found her this way!"

And then her own tears began to fall and fall some more. She began to ramble about all that Christina had told her in the morning about her dream, and how she felt so out of sorts being in the mix of people who were so disconsolate over the treatment they received and the fear for their future employment.

"She was a wreck, Detective, as you saw during your interrogation, and I came back here to try and help her through her fears."

Lydia sunk back to her knees, bloodied hands on her face, and sobbed in a way she never felt the need to do before. Her dear friend was dead. Her hated boss was dead. And who would be next?

"I'll have to take you to the stationhouse," he told Lydia in military fashion. "This time our interview will be away from your colleagues, and it will deal directly with what you have seen here in this room."

Without pause, the two walked out the door, leaving the room to the arriving forensics group to deal with Chris, her disfigured body, and the crime scene. It was time for Lydia to deal with her lack of knowledge of this crime, her aching head, and her own uncertain future.

Chapter Thirty

While sitting in the back of the patrol car driven by Guinness, Lydia thought of what it meant to become a lost soul on such a sunny day. Her dear friend had been murdered, and the police were not sure of her part in the event.

What *is* my part in this, she asked herself as the car glided down the highway. What am I doing here? Should I have been more protective of Christina? Should she have reported more of what she believed she saw when the police questioned us? What could I have done?

Lydia spoke up for the first time since leaving the scene of the crime.

"I need an icepack for my head," she said softly. "I fell back in the room, and I'm really hurting."

For the first time since she left Christina, she looked at her own hands and legs and could see the caked blood smeared all over her limbs and clothing. Bile rose in her throat as she tried to keep from vomiting.

The six miles to the police station took less than fifteen minutes, including two red lights on the way, but it felt like hours.

When they arrived at headquarters, she realized how lightheaded and weak she felt as her head continued to throb. How else could someone feel after coming across the dead body of a dear friend?

Once she looked down, she noticed again that she was still covered in dried blood. Her body trembled uncontrollably as Ruschak helped her slide out of the back seat. Isn't this where criminals sit when they are hoisted off to jail?

For once, however, she was thankful to have someone hold her by the elbow and escort her, even to the stationhouse where the imprint "Protect and Serve" rose in a dignified arch above the doorway.

Climbing the stairs to the entrance, she realized her legs and feet felt like they were weighed down by anchors. How would I feel if I was the one who really murdered her, Lydia wondered. Probably not as bad as I feel as the innocent person I am, who saw far too much.

Oh, God. How did this all happen? Who could have taken her life?

Lydia begged to go to a restroom to wash the blood off of her limbs. More so, she longed to go back to her room at the conference center to bathe and change clothing, but that all had to wait.

Ruschak, Guinness, and Lydia walked past the front desk and into an interview room. The small corner area held only a desk and two chairs. The walls were bare, save for one square window with vertical blinds that were snapped shut. The adjacent wall held the ubiquitous two-way mirror.

Ruschak quickly cleared the two chairs of the papers he had placed on them and motioned for Lydia to be seated.

I wonder who is on the other side of that mirror, thought Lydia. Ruschak is the only one with me in here, so Guinness must be there. And maybe others I don't even know.

Oh God.

Detective Ruschak sat on the edge of the table and placed his paper work on the chair next to hers. Why would he do that instead of the other way around?

"So Ms. Barrett, let's start at the beginning. Tell me about your time at Clearview Chemicals before we start to discuss Christina's murder."

He called her Christina and me by my last name. Is that procedure?

"I don't know where to begin, Detective," she answered quickly. "I've been employed by the company for three years, and Chris has been my friend and colleague in communications for all that time. I can't say it's been easy with her but…" She realized she was giving far more information than they needed or even wanted.

"What do you mean that it hasn't been easy?"

Lydia regretted those words as they seemed to designate Chris as a downright difficult person at any level.

"I didn't mean that she is a problem, but her lack of confidence is a chronic—I mean, it was a constant issue with her. I spent a great deal of time trying to buoy her spirits."

"So her problems must have gotten much worse with the Swaine's arrival," Ruschak stated, as if he already knew all the facts.

"Well, yes," replied Lydia. "She felt like her job was in jeopardy already, although she really was very good at it."

"That must have been difficult for you, as you had your own work to do and protect, Ms. Barrett."

Ruschak reached for his pen and pad of paper to make more notes and then asked, "What did you do before you worked at Clearview?"

Ruschak was perfunctory, matter of fact, and displayed less of the humanity he had at the conference center.

Is this the way an interrogation is always handled? Even though I haven't been Mirandized or told that I am a suspect?

Lydia decided to answer the questions the way she handled the media at work—with responses that were short and directly to the point.

"I was a journalist with a syndicated news source," she said, and no more. Then she changed her mind. "I got this job because of my former association as a member of the press."

"Why did you decide to move onto corporate communications, Ms. Barrett?"

"Could you please call me Lydia?" she pleaded. "The only Ms. Barrett I know is my mother. And shouldn't I be given the Miranda speech?"

Ruschak chuckled and shook his head from side to side. "No, that's not necessary at this time, Lydia. I really should try and put you at ease with this interview," he added. "You are not a person of interest, as of now. We just need to know what you saw and what you know about the events that led to Christina's death."

"I could never be considered as suspect! Never!"

Lydia's own ire caught her by surprise as she reacted to the idea that she could ever be considered a "person of interest."

"I'm only an innocent person who happened upon Christina in that state and tried my best to help her!" she shouted, and she looked at the two-way mirror to further articulate her position in the matter.

"Oh, I believe you, Lydia," said Ruschak more gently. "But we believe that you are the only one, except the murderer, who saw the crime scene in Christina's room before anyone else, and somehow you may not yet be aware of what the killer actually did."

Lydia relaxed. He believes me, she thought. Or is he just doing what cops do when they want to relax a perpetrator into revealing more than they choose? Perp. What a funny word.

Keep it short and simple, woman. Don't put yourself into an untenable position.

Then, without further thought, she said quickly and with too much enthusiasm, "I need to give you some more information that might help you with the investigation, Detective Ruschak." She continued, "I mean that I have a memory of something I heard Chris say when she thought she was dreaming during the night, about being outside in the parking lot that last night."

"Let's start from the beginning. You say that Chris said she was outside sometime during the night of Sunday, January fifth, and yet when I questioned everyone there, you said that," he pulled out his notebook and flipped through the pages. "She was 'shitfaced drunk,' and you were lucky that you and a friend got her back to her room before she puked and passed out in front of hundreds of people. Is that statement no longer true?"

Lydia actually started to laugh with the regretful remembrance of her friend, and Ruschak attempted to contain his own broad smile.

"It's true," said Lydia. "Damn it, whether you think it's funny or not, I do believe she did pass out after she threw up and Dean and I put her to bed. But I also believe that she got up again, perhaps to find her sleeping pills some time during the night. That's when she thought she went out to the parking lot that is adjacent to the building where we were staying.

"Maybe she decided to get some fresh air to clear her head. Maybe she just walked in that direction to get to me. You know my room is near the exit door. I don't know." Lydia sighed deeply and looked down at her discolored legs and torn stockings.

"Actually, I thought what she told me was just a dream until I noticed that the purple shoes she wore earlier that evening were all muddy. I don't think she had ever worn them before that evening, when we went to the cocktail lounge before dinner. She didn't step in any mud then, Detective. She walked only on the driveway blacktop between the hotel rooms and the Cromwell House.

"Anyway," Lydia continued, seemingly calmer for being heard without threat, "while she was outside, she said she heard a car door slam, and it occurred to her that someone she knew would see her out there, drunk. So she said she hid between the first two cars on the lot, but as she bent down, her pearl necklace caught on the side view mirror of one of the cars and ripped off of her neck. The pearls probably scattered in every direction."

"What does this have to do with the murder of Ms. Benderhoff?"

"Perhaps everything," Lydia replied. "She probably saw someone she knew get out of a car and run back through the hotel exit. And maybe that person saw her."

"People, for any reason, could have come into the hotel through that exit," replied Ruschak. "Why is what she saw so significant?"

"The person Chris saw had blood all over the front of whatever he or she was wearing—I know it now."

Lydia stopped, wiped her eyes with tissues, and continued. "When she told me the story this morning, she still thought it was just a dream. We both believed it was because she said she saw someone wearing a clown costume."

Ruschak looked squarely at Lydia in disbelief. "Why a clown costume?"

Lydia looked downward, head cocked to the side, and began to twist her fingers, feeling foolish as she told the story.

"Now that I think about it, I must sound like such an ass. Chris said the person had red blotches all up and down the front of the clothing, like a clown. It seemed like it must have been a costume until I thought about it in the morning. I think I know what she must have seen."

Ruschak began to pace. "Who was wearing the outfit with the red blotches, a man or a woman?"

"I really don't know," Lydia said softly, in real anguish. "I think I should be able to identify at least the gender of the person from what Chris told me. I vaguely remember Chris saying that the figure was small, but I swear I can't remember anything more. I hope you can pursue this further with the information I just gave you, Detective."

Ruschak had his back to Lydia as he looked out the window to the wooded landscape beyond. He turned slowly and said, "You have a good point, Ms. Barrett. Sorry, Lydia. It's something to consider." He turned and faced her as she noticed a look of respect on his face.

Detective Ruschak took a moment to think, then punched in numbers on his phone.

"It's me, Ruschak. Do you know the number of the psychiatrist, the regression specialist who uses hypnosis on police witnesses, Greg? We've used him before, and I don't have my file handy to look up his name."

He waited a moment longer, wrote down the name on the small notepad, adding the address and phone number of the doctor, said thanks, and hung up. He continued to write the information in what appeared to be a form of shorthand.

"Lydia, the guy we use is named Dr. Richard Gleason, and he's located here in Addison, near the center of town. I'm going to arrange for you to talk with him sometime very soon for some regression therapy. That is, if you're up to it." Lydia looked at Ruschak with curiosity.

Did he really think he could draw more information from me this way?

"And one more thing," he added, watching her reaction. The frightened woman tensed. "I have to admit that we did, in fact, know that Christina had been outside on Sunday evening. We have the pearls. They've been identified as Christina's by one of your colleagues. We found them scattered around the parking lot."

Ruschak pulled a plastic pouch out of his pocket containing a handful of the pale pink pearls and showed them to her.

Lydia finally bent her head forward and was reduced to wracking sobs. For the first time, Ruschak looked slightly uncomfortable.

"I understand how you feel, Ms. Barrett. You've lost a good friend in a horrible way," he said to her. "We'll return her pearls to you to give to a family member, after our investigation is complete. But for now, I have to hold onto them."

He walked over to Lydia and placed a gentle hand on her shoulder, tapping lightly. "Calm down, Lydia. We still have some work to do, and you need to have your wits about you.

"Now you can return to the conference center to clean up." Ruschak called out to Guinness, who was behind the glass plated window. "I'm going to take Ms. Barrett back to the conference center now, but one more thing," he added, turning back to Lydia. "Think hard. Did Christina give you any more information than what you told me now and what she revealed to us at the conference center?"

Lydia thought carefully about what Chris had said beyond what Swaine had unloaded on her the Friday before the conference. And she considered all that Christina had offered up in the morning.

"I don't think there's anything more, except one thing. Christina took sleeping pills every night because her anxiety left her sleepless without them."

Was that too much to add? Lydia thought it may have led to what Chris thought was a dream that night. She had to have gone out on the parking lot instead of dreaming about it. No doubt about it. So they have to know what might have influenced her beliefs.

"What type of sleeping pills did she take, Lydia?"

"I don't think she ever told me the name of the pills, but surely someone will find them in her room when your guys have completed the search of her things."

Ruschak walked to the door and called, "I'll be back in a minute or two. Just relax, Lydia."

Was he going to consider the relevance of the pills along with

Christina's statement? Lydia hoped so. She really hoped it has all to do with it, and Chris saw the real perp out on the lot. Perp! Now she was talking like the police on TV. But these guys were the real thing.

Ruschak returned as promised and said, "I'll take you back to your room now, Lydia. Here's my card." He reached into his wallet and pulled out an official card that showed his work phone and cell phone number.

"If you need me to take you back to the office, I'll wait in the lobby of the center. Your colleagues have been calling the stationhouse to tell us that they need you there to handle the media, and the other employees and have been anxious to talk to you." He stood, walked to the door, and opened it wide.

"Does this mean that you know I didn't have anything to do with Christina's death, Detective?"

"It looks that way, Lydia. But I must ask you not to discuss our conversation with anyone back at the site. What we learned from you is between us."

Ruschak reached out for Lydia's hand and helped her to stand and walk to the door.

"Thanks for the help, Detective," she said quietly. "I do need to bathe and change and get back to the office, and I do appreciate your kindness. But please," she said with a quavering voice, "find Christina's killer. I really don't care about Swaine, I'm sorry to say, but the two murders have to be connected."

Ruschak nodded sadly, noting the depth of Lydia's pain as he took hold of her elbow to escort her out of the interrogation room.

Chapter Thirty One

Several patrolmen, as well as Police Sergeant William Carmody of the investigation and forensics team, were waiting in the corridor outside of Lydia's office door when she arrived back at the site freshly washed and clothed.

After taking several aspirin tablets to ease her aching head and limbs, she felt no better. Her knees felt stiff and swollen, and the palms of her hands were rough and red from scrubbing the blood off. Worse still, her swollen eyes were partially shut from all the hysteria.

She could not get the sight of the blood washing down the shower drain out of her mind. It was such an entirely horrific experience, especially compared to the short time before when she had been in the water with Dean.

Down the hallway past her office, she noticed yellow security tape that read "Crime Scene—Do Not Cross" surrounding the room that Swaine had occupied for such a brief a period of time. A number of people, wearing blue jackets with "Forensics" written in yellow on the back, walked in and out of the area. Their feet were booted with disposable wraps so as not to disturb any hidden clues to Swaine's death.

Lydia still felt weak-kneed and uncomfortable. It had been at least thirty-six hours since the crime at the office had been committed, and then Christina's murder. Lydia began to cry loudly as she looked toward her friend's empty office.

"What's going on here?" she quickly asked Angela Guttierez, who stood waiting by Lydia's office door.

"Hi, Lydia. I'm so glad you're here."

Angela wrapped her arms around her boss and tried to comfort the stricken woman. When her arms and shoulders were wet to the core, Angela backed off and tried to tell Lydia what had transpired in Corporate Relations.

"I made a list of all the people who called to speak to you," said the agitated assistant. "I tried to get hold of you at the conference center, but they said you couldn't be reached. I'm really glad you came back here today. After I heard what happened to Christina, I wasn't sure if you'd be able to return so quickly."

She hugged her boss again, more tightly than before. Lydia viewed her assistant with great warmth. Angela Guttierez was always on top of her job, and this turn of events must have made her feel even more than unsettled, as displayed on her worried face.

"We'll have some time to discuss this whole horrible thing when I get finished talking with these gentlemen, Angie. And thank you, thank you," she said as evenly as she could, hoping that the trembling she continued to feel was not evident to everyone she would see on site.

"Would you please continue to take messages, and tell whoever calls that I'll be sure to get back to them later but I'm not sure when. Get all the numbers where they can be reached, but you already know the drill."

Angela nodded and watched Lydia enter her office, followed by Sergeant Carmody and a patrolman.

"Excuse me," Lydia said politely, as she quickly pulled out a TastyKake chocolate cupcake trio from a desk drawer and sat down to retrieve her voicemails.

The phone system automatically stamped the times as they were entered, as well as the name and extension number of the caller if they called from a location off the site.

With one finger held up to the policemen to wait a moment, she quickly jotted down the names and extensions of those inside the company who had left messages and the increasing number of calls from print and broadcast journalists in the surrounding area who had gotten word of the murders.

Turning quickly to the sergeant and the police officer standing in her doorway, she motioned them into her office to sit and talk.

"Care for a cupcake?" Lydia said offhandedly as she tried to get past her despair. The patrolman reached gratefully in the direction of Lydia's outstretched hand holding the confection, when his sergeant looked sourly in his direction. The officer pulled back his hand and looked away.

"Please have a seat," she said politely and sat down at her own desk.

"Listen, Ms. Barrett," said Sergeant Carmody, who remained standing. "I understand that you're the one who talks to the media around here. Detective Ruschak told me to brief you on what we believe happened here last night and at the conference center this afternoon so that you can decide how you and your company want to handle it."

The sergeant was about to launch into a full synopsis of what he knew of the killings that was open for public consumption when Lydia suggested that he call in Karen as well.

"She's got to pass the same information on to our employees, more than 2,000 of them, and the information that I offer to the media should not differ in any way from what she says."

"Where is this woman?" asked the sergeant.

"She's right down the hallway. I'll call her." Lydia picked up her phone and punched in Karen's extension.

Obviously grateful to be included, Karen appeared at Lydia's door within seconds of receiving the call.

The sergeant looked at the two young women, both in their thirties— one dark-haired with a healthy, rose-colored complexion, the other blond, and far more glamorous—good window dressing for a company that wants decent public exposure, he thought.

"Okay, ladies," he began in a fatherly tone. "What I have to tell you is not prettied up for delicate ears. It's what really happened to this guy Swaine and your colleague, Ms. Benderhoff. What you have to do is pass on as little as necessary to satisfy the media and the basic requirements of the other employees.

"You know, it's not our policy to reveal all the facts as we discover them. It can loosen up our case against the perpetrator, once we identify him."

The women looked at one another. "Well, Sergeant," said Karen officiously, "tell us all you can."

The sergeant motioned to the patrolman, who stood next to him to close the door. The office, constructed to hold far fewer people than who now occupied it, felt close and airless.

"Get your pens ready, ladies, here are the facts." Sergeant Carmody swung open his own notebook, leafed through several pages, and settled on one.

"The remains of one R.B. Swaine were discovered by his assistant, a Miriam Ashworth, at 11:10 this morning. In the statement made by Ms. Ashworth before she was admitted to the Addison Medical Center with chest pains, she said that Mr. Swaine's door was closed when she arrived in the early morning. She also said that she had only worked with him here at this site for a few days and that she didn't feel comfortable about disturbing him while he was so involved with his work."

The sergeant leafed through a few more pages, settled again on one, and continued. "Ms. Ashworth said that he didn't answer any of his phone calls, which automatically bounced to her line after four rings.

"The deceased's wife called three times before Ms. Ashworth finally answered his phone and decided it was time to disturb him." The sergeant shifted uneasily on his feet. "This part, ladies, is not for the squeamish," he said, looking to see if the two women were prepared for the graphic details.

"The assistant claims she opened the door and found Mr. Swaine slumped over his desk. At first, she thought he had become sick, and she immediately checked his pulse. Ms. Ashworth concluded that as soon as she touched his skin she knew that he was dead, and she ran out of the office. Another assistant, the one with the cubicle next to Ms. Ashworth…" Carmody checked his notes again. "Her name is Angela Guttierez."

"She's my assistant, the woman just outside this door," Lydia said quickly, now more puzzled than before. Carmody looked up from his notes at Lydia, paused briefly, and continued.

"The Guttierez woman said she saw Ms. Ashworth's reaction and ran to see what was wrong. Ms. Guttierez said that she looked in the office and saw Swaine hanging over the desk. She turned back just in time to see Ms. Ashworth collapse. That Guttierez woman is a fast thinker," he mentioned with admiration.

"So Ms. Guttierez first checked Swaine to see if he was conscious, and she saw that he was dead. Then she called the emergency services here at the site. You people obviously know that there are a bunch of volunteers in every area of each building who are trained in first aid and CPR, in addition to the nurses at the Health Services Department.

He stopped to take a breath. "Well, they came running and saw that Ms. Ashworth was having trouble breathing, so they called the local ambulance corps. They got here in short order, and away she went."

Lydia interjected, "But how is she now?"

"She's in the cardiac care unit of the Addison Medical Center, and on last report she was resting comfortably and being carefully monitored. If you're thinking of visiting, I must advise you not to talk about the case with her. We haven't had a chance to fully debrief her, and any information about the case that you discuss with her must be cleared through us first."

Karen, leaning forward in her seat, asked the officers, "Well, what actually happened to Mr. Swaine? How did he die?"

The sergeant looked directly at Karen and replied, "He was struck with a blunt instrument. The actual weapon and the location of the injury I cannot divulge to you. You understand, don't you? It's departmental policy."

"But, Sergeant," pleaded Lydia, "you must be able to give us more to offer than that. Was he killed instantly, was there a struggle, or was he caught by surprise? Do you think he knew his killer? Surely you can give us that much."

"I'm sorry, Miss." The sergeant looked at his notebook again and said, "Ms. Barrett, I mean. But you don't need that information to talk to the media, or you, Ms. Paulson, to the other employees. As I said before, this is an ongoing investigation. We don't know all the facts yet."

"Well, then just tell us, what is the estimated hour of his death? Were there any people who saw him here last evening? Was he seen with anyone?"

"Are you some kind of detective, Ms. Barrett?" The policeman asked, an amused smile gracing his face. "You want to be the one who solves the crime?" The policemen looked at one another and laughed out loud.

"I don't have any idea of how a crime is investigated or solved," Lydia replied coldly. "I just want to be prepared when the media asks me the same things I'm asking you and I'm forced to stand there with a dumb look on my face."

"All you have to say," said the sergeant in a more kindly tone "is that Swaine was struck with a blunt object, which has been tentatively identified by the police. The time of death is placed between eight and ten last evening. His body was discovered shortly before noon today by his assistant, who, shocked by the discovery, suffered a cardiac event. Currently, she is resting comfortably at Addison Medical Center. She has not yet been questioned by the police, due to her condition, and she is under police protection to prevent her from being disturbed while she is being treated."

"Well, what about his family?" asked Karen. "Doesn't he have a wife and children?"

"His wife was immediately notified. Actually, she had called his assistant several times during the morning, but I told you that before.

"Ms. Ashworth apparently told her his door was closed and he couldn't be disturbed. His children, by the way, both teenagers, are hers by a prior marriage. From the first reports, it seems as though he wasn't any too popular at home either."

"What do you mean by that, Sergeant?" asked Karen directly. "Are you implying that perhaps a member of his own family could have killed him?"

"Not likely," said Carmody. "Mrs. Swaine has been in New Hampshire with the children, completing the sale of their house before they could join him here. I believe she's on her way down here now to identify her husband's body and make arrangements. I expect we'll be seeing her soon.

"With the forensic team in place, we'll have more answers, too. Some in a few hours, the rest in a few days. This I can say for sure: it was no accident. The person who killed that son of a bitch really wanted him dead."

"Why do you say that, Sergeant?" asked Karen.

The sergeant began to answer her, but thought better of it and replied, "The condition of the body, ma'am. I can't tell you more, but the killer didn't leave anything to chance."

The women looked at each other and Karen shuddered.

"Sorry, ladies, I didn't mean to upset you, but you wanted details and that's all I can give you to go on now."

Linda Spear

"And what about the details of Christina's death?" Lydia asked quietly, tears again filling her eyes. "I need to know what you've discovered so far."

"We don't have much to tell you yet, but here are the pictures," Carmody said succinctly. "When we know, we'll give you all the details of what we've found."

Lydia took a brief look at the bloody ruin of her friend on his tablet, and rose from her seat while asking to go to the bathroom to be sick.

The men were clearly not surprised by her reaction, and Carmody said, "Of course."

But Lydia managed to withhold the urge to be sick and sat down again. Instead, she sipped from her water bottle that she had brought with her to work.

"Okay," she said quietly. "I'm fine now. May I make a few calls to the media, Sergeant? I need to arrange a press conference, and I want to get this information to them fast before they begin to print their own suppositions as to what happened, just to fill newspaper space. After that, I need to talk to our Chief Executive Officer, Charles Wainwright."

"Certainly, miss," said the sergeant obligingly. "I'm well aware of what a pain in the butt those media types can be." As he headed for the door, he turned his head and said sternly, "Don't give them any opinions, miss. Remember, give them just the information that we decided was necessary."

Karen politely edged by the policemen and mumbled her apologies. She was back in her own office before Lydia could ask her how she planned to convey the information to the employees.

More concerned with the job at hand, Lydia methodically called the Audiovisual Tech Department on site to have a podium and microphone set up in the main lobby no later than 3:45 in the afternoon. She also urged them to do a comprehensive sound check, as the crowd before her would be huge and would produce noise of their own.

With Angela's help, she contacted the heads of all departments at the company, each communication source via email, making sure that everyone would be at the right place at the right time.

The lobby location, she believed, would allow for security to monitor activity within the building and keep outside traffic to a standstill.

Employees, she learned, had already been asked by Paul Frenkle to remain in the vicinity of their offices for the day in order to facilitate the police investigation.

By 3:15 in the afternoon, having completed these arrangements, Lydia walked down the hall toward Macomber's office to tell him her plans for the press conference and to ask him to be present. The police officers standing by the entrance to the dead man's office, located next to Macomber's, asked her reason for being in the area.

"I need to talk with my boss, Mr. Macomber," she said, not mentioning that Dean's office, just past Macomber's and directly across from Swaine's, was her next stop.

Lydia entered Macomber's office and found him sifting through files piled high on his desk. Her boss looked up indifferently and motioned for Lydia to be seated. She noticed that a large stack of straws were clearly visible atop his desk, and one was prominently protruding from his mouth.

"I'm looking through Swaine's papers, Lydia, the ones the police didn't take. He apparently had a stack of material on his desk that they impounded, but these are the few that he had stacked outside his office next to Miss Ashworth's desk. They are all Human Resource files about each corporate employee and their most recent evaluations. He wasn't leaving anything to chance.

"Don't you think it's possible that I could come up with some information that will help the police nail the killer this way?"

Linda Spear

Lydia noticed the apprehension in his voice. Did Macomber look panicked, or was it just her overactive imagination?

"I'm sure the police will want to see everything that Swaine has collected regarding the employees since he's been here, Dan. Have you told them that you have some of his files?"

Macomber looked surprised. "No, I haven't told them about these files yet. I'll give them over to Ruschak after I finish with them."

Lydia said nothing. Was Macomber looking to cover up something he believed could be found in Swaine's files? Was there something in there that he believed could involve him in the investigation?

"I think you better finish up with those files, fast, Dan. It's not a good idea to be holding on to potential evidence."

Daniel pushed the files away with disgust and leaned back in his chair, chewing frantically on his straw.

"Lydia, I'm scared that Swaine had begun a termination file on me. If he started to document how my role could be eliminated and absorbed by him, the police are going to stick like glue until they find something to pin on me. I know it."

"Why would you say that, Dan? You weren't anywhere near this place last night, were you?"

"No, but I don't have anyone to say that I wasn't here. None of us who were alone in our rooms can prove it, even you, Lydia."

"Relax," she replied. "The police are savvy enough to know that Swaine had to be killed by someone who must have had a far more compelling reason to want him dead. Granted," she continued, as if she were talking to an audience, "lots of people, besides you, hated him. But most people who are hated are not killed, unless they ticked off just the precise pathological personality. The victim, in this case, Swaine, may have been in the wrong place at the wrong time, or maybe he threatened the killer or a loved one's life. And that's probably why Christina was killed too." Lydia looked directly at her boss and added, "Dan, you simply don't fit into any of those categories."

"Do you think the police will understand that, Lydia?"

"Sure, Dan, sure, but I came in to tell you the details of the press conference scheduled for four this afternoon. Crews are setting up the AV equipment and the podium in the main lobby, which is flanked by security guards so that no one gets past the front entrance. I think you should be there. What do you think?"

Macomber continued to examine the files and raised his head again only to say, "Yeah, I think that's a good idea. What time did you say, again?

"Four o'clock, in the main lobby."

"I'll be there," he mumbled and continued to probe the assorted mess on his desk. Lydia turned and left the office without saying goodbye. She knew it wouldn't be heard.

When she finally entered the cordoned off space, after waiting patiently through a handbag and briefcase search by the police at the entrance, they checked the section of their entryway to see if Detective Ruschak had arrived. Sergeant Carmody, the man who had supplied the information for her prepared statement at the press conference, told her that the detective was inside Swaine's office and motioned her through.

Ruschak sat behind Swaine's desk, drawers open and papers spread over every flat surface. Ruschak was a man far shorter than Swaine; he looked diminished by the furniture around him. The desk and chair were custom made and scaled to suit the size of the man who initially filled the space.

Although the office had been obviously dusted for fingerprints and returned to a reasonable state of normalcy, the carpet, stained with rust-

Linda Spear

colored blotches, still displayed the result of the ghastly crime.

"What's up, Lydia?" He waved casually, in a seemingly happy gesture to see her again.

"I'm heading back down to my office to do the final prep on the statement for the media. Gotta run."

"Before you do, Lydia, we can't get you an appointment with Dr. Gleason until next week. He's away on a skiing trip."

Lydia didn't know whether to feel relief or despair, as the thought of hypnotic recall made her even more squeamish. What would it reveal that could implicate people that matter to me, she wondered. Shouldn't it have been Chris who got that invitation to the shrink's office?

Oh Chris...

Ruschak nodded and said, "Just so you know. I'll give you the heads up when the appointment is made." He looked back down at his work.

Lydia felt relieved as she walked back down the hallway and reentered her own office. She closed the door and threw her purse on the desk, where she noticed the blinking light of her voicemail. Message one she found was again from her sister who, concerned that she hadn't heard from Lydia in several days, requested an immediate call back.

Message two was from extension 7515—Dean's office. "I miss you already," his voice said. "I stopped into your office to see you this morning, but you weren't in yet. Since you left me hours ago in my room, I haven't been able to think of anything else but us. Actually, the only thing that's keeping me going today is that I know I'll see you tonight. Stop at my office later, if you can," the message said.

A half-dozen other messages were from members of the media, who asked for updates, left call back numbers, or mentioned that they would call again.

The last message was from Angela.

"Lydia, you know that I was asked to handle Miriam's mail and phone calls for now, and that's fine," the message began. "I found something that was sent to her through the interoffice mail that I don't understand. Please let me know when you get in. That is, if you are coming in today. I need to show this to you."

Lydia, with a face still swollen and red from tears, lifted the receiver to return Angela's call when she was startled by a forceful knock on her door. Without waiting for an answer from within, Detective Ruschak opened the door and walked in. Lydia replaced the phone receiver.

"I realize how busy you are," he said almost apologetically, "but I want to talk with you privately."

Lydia looked at the detective with bewilderment.

"Please have a seat, Detective," she said quietly.

"Christina was lucky to have a friend like you," he said. "We knew she wasn't guilty of any wrongdoing from the start, but she was so nervous about the situation that you and your group found yourselves in that I was concerned about her at the interrogation earlier this afternoon."

Lydia looked closely at the detective's face and was mildly surprised to see more emotion than a police officer would ordinarily display in the context of his work.

Aware that Lydia regarded him curiously, he quickly reverted to his original facade of objectivity.

"What else did you find out when you questioned the night housekeeper?" he asked. "Apparently she wasn't on duty when we questioned the other conference center staff members yesterday."

Just then, Ruschak's cell phone rang. Ruschak listened carefully to the person at the other end of the line and said, "We figured that was about the time. Tell me something I don't know."

Again he fell silent as he listened intently. Suddenly his vacant expression turned to surprise as he blurted out, "Twice? Are you sure of that? Good job, Doc. Have the formal sealed report sent to my desk. I'll read it all later."

"Is there a problem, Detective?" asked Lydia, now more curious than before. "I take it that was the medical examiner."

"You're a very perceptive woman," Ruschak said with obvious respect. "I'm sure you've figured out the entire conversation from what you've overheard me say."

"All but one thing," Lydia replied. "You said, 'twice?' I don't know what that refers to."

Ruschak hesitated, then looked Lydia square in the eye and said, "Perhaps someday I'll tell you, but now it's squarely in our hands. All of our suppositions were just confirmed by the ME regarding Swaine's death. He did, however, add something we didn't know. I'm not sure if this factor will be of any ultimate importance, but I would appreciate it if you do not mention any conversations you've overheard or what you surmise to your colleagues or anyone else."

"You have my word, Detective," Lydia said with all sincerity.

"Thanks. Now back to the subject of the night maid." Lydia went on to tell Ruschak everything that had transpired back at the conference center when she and Christina tracked down the housekeeper who had helped Christina return to her room.

"That's powerful information you've given me, Lydia, and I'm grateful for your assistance."

Ruschak appeared energized by the additional information, and as he quickly turned to the doorway, he said, "Thanks," and paused. "Not everyone wants to support police efforts, you know. I appreciate your candor."

As Ruschak walked back down the corridor, Lydia quickly punched in Angela's extension.

"I know that today will be a real bummer with the media and all, but listen. I have to show you something that was sent to Swaine and arrived in Miriam's mail. Can I bring it down to you now?"

"Sure, I'm here."

Within seconds, Angela appeared at the door with a manila file folder in her hand. "Look at this," she said, thrusting the file into Lydia's hands.

"Angie, I'd love to look at all of this now, but I have to get to the press conference in just a few minutes. I can see from my window that the front of the building is already packed. So just save that material for me until I come back."

Angela sighed with resignation as she put the file down on Lydia's desk before she returned to her own seat.

Lydia quickly walked down the hall to where the offices at the end were cordoned off with police tape. In the office next door to Swaine's office, she saw Dean seated at his desk. Without reporting to the police, who watched her movements, she entered Dean's office and attempted to close the door.

From the corner of her eye, she could see one of the patrolmen guarding the crime scene. He approached Dean's office and politely asked her to leave the door open. Lydia swung the door back against the wall, and the patrolman quickly resumed his post at the entry to Swaine's office.

As Lydia turned to face Dean, she noticed his left hand was tapping his desk nervously. His right hand rose to his forehead, and he began to rub his brow as he repeatedly licked his lips. Dean Handlesman was in an agitated state. He motioned her to sit down and stared into her face in

Linda Spear

anticipation. Lydia began.

"I just wanted to tell you that the press conference is scheduled for four this afternoon, about a half hour from now, and I thought you'd want to be there."

Dean seemed to relax. He reached to touch her, when Lydia's eyes darted out to the hallway. Dean retracted his hand and placed it back on his desk.

"I haven't been briefed by the police about what happened here like you have," he told her, "so I don't know what issues could be brought up by the media."

Lydia quickly told Dean what little she knew about how Swaine had died. She also mentioned the fact that Paul Frenkle and Cal Ferguson had conducted an indoor air quality check during that whole weekend, including the evening of the murder.

"That fact, if it gets out to the media, could conjure up some questions that you'd be one of the best ones to handle."

"Well, what did Frenkle and Ferguson find?" Dean asked, alarmed.

"Actually, I haven't been briefed on that yet. I know they checked for chemical contaminants, both indoor and outdoor, that could have been trapped in the venting systems. They even tested the carpeting for toxicity. From what I haven't heard so far, there was probably nothing of major significance."

"Well then, isn't that something you can say without additional verification?"

Lydia stared at Dean, surprised at his lack of interest in presenting the facts to the media on his own.

"It's your field, Dean. I can say what needs to be said, but you know that the media likes to attribute facts of this sort to the person responsible for knowing the most about them."

Dean sensed her annoyance and sat forward in his chair. "Of course, I'll report the findings if I'm asked. I'll call Frenkle and Ferguson first to get the information." He looked squarely at Lydia. "Please forgive me for not thinking fast today. I think sitting so near that poor dead schmuck's office has left me unglued."

Lydia looked at him sympathetically. "I guess I'm lucky to be situated down the hall. I don't have to literally look at what happened here last night."

"By the way," started Dean with renewed interest. "Did Frenkle and Ferguson see anything strange last night? Do you think they know more about this than we do?"

"It appears not," Lydia replied. "They said that they knew that Swaine was in his office because his light was on, but they didn't want to bother him."

"Lucky for us," he said guardedly.

"Why do you say that?"

"Because if they found his body last night and if the murder was reported to the police immediately, we would have been notified last night." Dean moved uncomfortably in his chair. His face grew fearful. "Think of the explaining you and I would have had to do."

Chapter Thirty-Two

The main lobby of Clearview Chemicals and the stairway down to the street below was jam-packed long before four, when the press conference was scheduled to begin. Members of the media, equipped with Steadicams, digital tape recorders, iPads, and Surface tablets, were surrounded by local townspeople, members of the business community, and a large contingent of shocked employees. Lydia made her way to the podium and microphone, meeting Charles B. Wainwright on the way.

"All set, Lydia?"

"As set as I'm going to be," she replied decisively. "Are you still square with the plan for me to make the initial remarks about Swaine's murder and to let you take over to eulogize the man and Christina?"

"I think that's the best way. Let's get on with it," he mumbled, and he consulted an index card on which he appeared to have jotted a few notes. Lydia stepped up to the microphone, tested it for volume, and adjusted its height.

"Welcome, men and women of the media, friends, Clearview employees, and others who have joined us today. I am sure you have already heard that Robert Benjamin Swaine, Vice President, Administration, was found dead in his office before noon today. The cause of his death is still under investigation, but he appears to have been slain by a blow to the head with a blunt object.

"Although the exact time of his death is still somewhat uncertain, the police believe that he died between the hours of eight and ten last night. His body was found this morning by his secretary, Miriam Ashworth. Unfortunately, Ms. Ashworth was apparently overcome by shock, and she suffered what her doctors believe to be a myocardial infarction. In other words, a heart attack.

"I understand that she is resting comfortably at the Addison Medical Center, and I've been instructed to tell you that she cannot receive visitors or phone calls at this time. She is currently under police guard to ensure her medical progress. All efforts are being made by the Addison police to identify Mr. Swaine's assailant.

"You may not have heard about the subsequent death of Christina Benderhoff, a communications specialist associated with our group. She was stabbed to death while we met at the nearby East Forge Conference Center, by a person or persons unknown."

Loud chatter and groans arose from the crowd at the newest bit of information, and Lydia had to yell into the microphone for everyone to cease so she could continue with her statement.

"I know this is shocking news to you all, and we are as surprised and overwhelmed as you may feel, but all of those associated with Clearview Chemicals are doing their utmost to assist the police in this matter.

"That is all I have to say at this time. Our Chief Executive Officer, Mr. Charles B. Wainwright, would like to say a few words before we accept your questions. Mr. Wainwright?"

Wainwright stepped up to the microphone and put the index card in his suit jacket pocket. He nervously fingered the microphone to raise it to the level of his face.

Before he could begin speaking, a voice from the crowd called out, "Who do you think did the crimes, Mr. Wainwright? Both by the same person?"

Wainwright, baffled by the intensity of the onlookers, gazed in the direction of the remark and said, "It's not for me to surmise. I'll leave that to the police," and then he began his discourse on the laudable career of Robert B. Swaine.

Wainwright detailed Swaine's stellar history as a renowned strategic planner in the corporate community and how lucky he believed Clearview Chemicals was to have acquired his services for the company. He mentioned

Swaine's grieving wife and children, and chose to omit that he had not yet contacted them with condolences.

He spoke of Swaine's mission and Christina's capabilities, then expressed his own regrets that the job would now be done by those probably less able.

Sooner than Lydia realized, Wainwright was through, standing uncertainly before the microphone. He looked in Lydia's direction, and she quickly joined him at the podium, searching the crowd for Dean, Daniel, or any of the other communicators who could add support. No one who was expected had arrived in the lobby yet.

Then the questions began in earnest.

"Ms. Barrett, Chuck Forrest, AP. Neither you nor Mr. Wainwright has mentioned motives. Have any been established yet by the police?"

"Mr. Forrest, the police have only just begun their investigation. I feel sure that when they have completed their preliminary questioning, they will be able to offer some insight into the motive."

A face in the crowd, finally recognizable to Lydia, jumped up and down in the crowd demanding to be seen and heard. "Valerie Teague, the Addison Sentinel, Lydia," she said familiarly. "Does your management think these are random acts of violence or targeted killings?"

Lydia looked for help from the police who were ringing the area to prevent the crowd from getting out of hand. She noticed Detective Ruschak to her far left and behind Wainwright, and she motioned for him to join her at the microphone. "I think that question can best be addressed by a member of the police force. Detective Ruschak?"

Ruschak pushed his way to the podium and took the mike into his hand. "No need to worry about a crazy person running around killing people in town, Miss," he began. "The person or persons who attacked Swaine and Christina Benderhoff were not looking to kill indiscriminately. They were murdered for a reason or reasons as yet unknown. As soon as we have more facts, we'll be able to share them with the media."

"Steven Talarico, the East Forge Herald," called out a young man who had pushed his way to the front of the crowd. "I understand, Mr. Wainwright, that a number of the people who worked for Mr. Swaine were attending a meeting at the East Forge Conference Center when the murder occurred. Are they being looked at as possible suspects since they worked for the man and were so close to the site when the murder occurred?"

Wainwright looked uncomfortable as he gazed over at Lydia, as if to ask her if she would take the question. Lydia remained immobile.

"As the detective stated, as yet, the police have no knowledge of a motive and, therefore, cannot pinpoint possible suspects as of yet. All I can say is that anyone who has had recent contact with Mr. Swaine has indeed been questioned by the police, including me." With a pretense of lighthearted humor, Wainwright added, "And I can tell you that I didn't commit the crime."

Lydia wished she had taken Wainwright up on his silent plea. This was no time for an attempt at humor. She stepped up to the microphone, and Wainwright gratefully retreated.

"One more question, people," Lydia stated firmly.

"Soundgarten," came a voice from the crowd. "New York Times. We have some information about Mr. Swaine that was quite unflattering. Are there any employees or family members of his who are now under suspicion?"

"Where did you get the notion that Mr. Swaine was unpopular around here?" Lydia asked firmly.

Soundgarten just shrugged and said, "I take it that inference about him is correct, Ms. Barrett, unless you can tell me otherwise."

Lydia bit down hard on her lower lip, and with all the professionalism she could bring to the subject, she said, "That supposition, Mr. Soundgarten, is just speculation. I cannot acknowledge any animosity among the ranks as of this press conference. As the police gain more information, no doubt you will have an answer to your question."

That's when she knew that the party was over and said to the restless crowd, "At this time, people, I'm calling this press conference to a close. As more information becomes available to us, we will certainly convey the facts to you. Thank you again for coming."

Lydia shut off the microphone and walked away as a number of people from the crowd pushed forward and continued to pitch questions in her direction that she chose to disregard. She could feel Wainwright's presence as he followed her closely like a lost puppy, and Ruschak took up the rear of the small procession.

As they entered the hallway of the executive area, Wainwright leaned against a wall. Cold sweat appeared on his pale face and forehead, and his lower lip trembled.

"Was it hot out there, or is it just me?" he asked neither Lydia nor the detective as he loosened his collar and tie. Wainwright suddenly looked quite old.

"It was close in there, Mr. Wainwright, and you were under a lot of pressure. Perhaps you should go back to your office and lay down on your couch for a while, until you feel better."

She cradled his right elbow, and he allowed himself to be led to his office door where he was met at the entrance by Kay McIntosh, his assistant, who quickly took his arm and just as hastily closed the door. Ruschak and Lydia stood in silence as they were left in the hallway in such haste.

Lydia knocked on the door and waited for Ms. McIntosh to open it. Once she did, the scene in the CEO's office was filled with turmoil.

"I hired that man!" they heard Wainwright shout out to no one in particular. "I caused his death by bringing him here, and the death of Christina must be tied to it," he added mournfully.

Stretched out on the couch in his office was a broken soul. Charles B. Wainwright had aged many years in one day. His left forearm was thrown across his eyes, and his weeping did not stop. Kay tried to lift a glass of water to his lips, but he brushed her away, sending the glass flying.

"It's my fault, my entire fault," he said. "It's as if I murdered the two of them myself. If only I had let my employees do the job they were called on to do, we would still have a well-functioning company."

His soliloquy went on and on. Kay stood ramrod straight next to her boss, and Ruschak was quickly capturing all of what was said in his notebook. Lydia just stared in horror.

Yes, she thought, terrible things had happened to them over the period of several days, and Wainwright should accept the blame for bringing such a man to their company. Lydia shook her head sadly. He should have kept his hands out of our department. Then we would have Christina back and no Swaine in sight. Imagine. We could have continued to work in peace.

Ruschak spoke to Wainwright for the first time since they entered his office. "Could you please tell me why you consider yourself responsible for this tragedy?"

Wainwright shot up on the couch to a sitting position, yanked the wet cloth that covered his forehead, and threw it in the direction of Ruschak. Then he shrieked, "Get out of here! I didn't invite you in. This is not your problem; it's mine. Go away!"

Kay hastened to pick up the wet cloth and tried to excuse her boss' behavior. "He's just not well," she mumbled, almost bending before the policeman in an act of contrition.

The two interlopers realized there was no opportunity to gain further information from the broken man, so they quietly walked out of the office as Kay McIntosh slowly closed the door. Lydia and Ruschak turned left at the next corridor and headed back in the direction of her office.

"It sounds like he's taking a real beating over this one," Detective Ruschak said to Lydia. "He must feel awful. He really was the one responsible for pursuing Swaine and bringing him on board. But who in their right mind would kill Christina?"

Lydia and Ruschak turned away from the CEO's office and walked down the hallways while looking at prize-winning works of art that graced the corridors of the executive suite of offices.

As they made their way back to the corporate relations area, Ruschak looked to his side and asked, "What is your take on Swaine's hire and, if you want to be a smart ass about it, his quick firing?"

"Detective, I'm really tired out now. I don't have anything more to say to anyone about this. Don't you think the press conference was enough? If you're trying to see if I had any personal interest in who Mr. Wainwright hired, you are going about it in the wrong way. Ask me anything you want tomorrow when I've had a night's sleep, but don't try to bullshit me now."

Ruschak smiled knowingly. "Swaine, from all accounts, was a total bastard. I didn't expect you to paint me a different picture, but I wanted to know if you were as seriously concerned about his presence here as some of your colleagues. I also hoped you could shed some light on who might have had the biggest reason for wanting him and Christina dead."

Lydia, decidedly more guarded now, said, "If I had any inkling, Detective, I'd surely mention it, but please remember that I just began dealing with it a few hours ago. I haven't had any time to talk at length with my colleagues, and I don't know if we'll have a chance to discuss it at all in the next few days. It's likely to stay pretty busy for all of us around here, and I really need some sleep."

Lydia stopped in her tracks and said, "But I do want to be kept apprised of who will take responsibility for Christina's body and what arrangements will be made after the coroner's office is through with their work. That's what matters to me. The whole thing is just too overwhelming for me to think clearly now."

When the detective and Lydia had arrived back to her office area, Ruschak said, "I'll be glad to keep you updated on that score, Lydia, but what I want you to do is keep your eyes and ears open to conversation at the conference center tonight.

"One of the reasons I asked all of you who were attending the conference at East Forge to return there tonight is because I want you and your colleagues to talk to each other, and your job is to listen.

"With luck, perhaps you'll be able to produce some fresh insight into the case. So if you don't mind, I'll be checking with you again tomorrow when you return here in the morning."

Lydia felt trapped. He wants me to grill my friends for a possible motive, she thought. He's also out of his fucking mind.

After she thanked him for escorting her back to her office, she sat down at her desk.

"See you tomorrow, Ms. Barrett," called out the detective as he turned to leave.

"Remember, Detective. The name is Lydia," she called after him as he headed back down toward the cordoned off section that contained Swaine's office and Dean's.

Ruschak nodded. "Remembered, Lydia," and he walked away with a half-smile.

Lydia intended to phone Dean, rather than walk into his office under the scrutiny of the detective and his staff, but as she lifted the receiver, she noticed the sealed envelope in the center of her desk that Angie had said was so important before the press conference. Angie was gone for the day, so she didn't have the ability to ask her why it was so imperative that she see it right away.

The thin file was from Human Resources. On the lip was the name, "Karen Paulson/AKA/Anne Karen Diamond." Inside the file were documents that read:

Employee File #44923

Name: Karen Paulson

/AKA/

Anne Karen Diamond

Address: Three Avian Heights, Apartment 8G

Addison, New York

Job Title: Manager, Internal Communications

Date of Hire: September, 2000

Last Known Employer: Andrus Chemicals

Jamestown, New Hampshire

Recommendations: Ronald Weymart, CEO Andrus Chemicals
Arnold Breuer, V.P. Corporate
Communications
Robert B. Swaine, V.P. Administration

Robert Swaine! Lydia sat back in her seat, dumbfounded. She continued to leaf through the file. Along with the statistical information regarding Karen's base salary, yearly increases, benefits package, investment savings plan, physical exam, and drug test results that deemed her fit for full-time employment, were the notations made by the Human Resource employee who interviewed Karen upon application for her job.

Included in the file were the recommendations forwarded from her previous employer. Lydia focused on the recommendation of Robert B. Swaine.

June, 2009

To Whom It May Concern:

Anne Diamond is an eminently capable communicator. Her organizational skills, coupled with her willingness to meet new challenges head on, have made her an asset to our company.

Unfortunately, a restructure of several of our corporate departments has forced us to relieve some valued employees of their positions. Anne is one such person. Her creative talents will surely be missed.

Sincerely,

Robert B. Swaine

Lydia closed the file and sat leaden at her desk. If they knew one another—Karen and Swaine—why did they pretend otherwise? When did Karen—Anne—change her name?

Lydia felt another sudden wave of lightheadedness. Her heart was racing uncontrollably, and her hands tingled. Why was the file delivered to Miriam Ashworth on Monday morning? Who ordered it? Ashworth or Swaine himself?

What the hell is going on here?

Lydia stood, feeling somewhat disoriented, and sat down again. The file was something she knew belonged in Ruschak's possession, but she cautioned herself. What would Ruschak do with this material? Question Karen? Question Lydia, once again, about her possession of the file? What did any of our Human Resources files reveal about us?

With increasing hesitation, Lydia rose again and headed in the direction of Swaine's office, the file folder under her arm.

Standing before the office, surrounded by the yellow crime scene tape, was Sergeant Guinness. He nodded politely to Lydia as she attempted to shimmy under the yellow tape.

"Not so fast, miss," he cautioned. "What's the nature of your business in this office?"

Annoyed by his formality, Lydia sighed heavily and said lightly, "I just have to speak with Detective Ruschak about something I remembered." Her need to speak to him had nothing to do with memory but everything to do with what she held in her hand, and she wished to present it to him personally.

Guinness peered into the office, and Lydia followed his glance. Ruschak was engrossed in a phone call, head down, appearing to look through the massive desk where he sat. In his other hand was Swaine's gold pen, which he twirled lightly between two fingers.

Guinness motioned to Ruschak, hoping to catch his attention. Ruschak failed to look up, and Guinness once again faced Lydia, shrugging nonchalantly.

"I guess you'll have to wait till he's done, miss."

Getting increasingly irritated, Lydia asked, "Has he been on the phone long? Will he be off soon?"

Guinness again shrugged. "Beats me. Looks like it's important, so I can't even take a guess."

Lydia shook her head with annoyance, and with file in hand, she headed in the direction of her office. She looked again into Christina's empty office and recalled all over again the pain of the crime scene in Cromwell House and the tragic loss of her friend. Then she looked diagonally across the hall and saw that Dean was in animated conversation with Randy Goddard.

Without anyone available to consult with about the file, she decided to return to her own office to wait—and think.

Chapter Thirty-Three

Lydia intended to phone Dean, rather than walk back to his office under the scrutiny of the detective and his staff, but as she lifted the receiver, she noticed the blinking light that indicated that she had messages waiting for her on the phone system.

The first message was from her sister in Philadelphia, recorded at noon. She wanted to know if Lydia was all right and if she had received the latest shipment of TastyKake Butterscotch Krimpets and chocolate cupcakes.

The second message was in the form of a broadcast message from Karen Paulson, time stamped at 2:30 that afternoon. It blanketed all phones on site. Karen had apparently decided to use this means to communicate the latest information about the murders to all employees. Broadcast messages through text messages, she knew, was a quicker, more efficient way to communicate any emergency situation that affected the over two thousand people at company headquarters. Karen's message began:

"This is Karen Paulson, Manager of Communications at the Addison site of Clearview Chemicals."

As if they didn't know, thought Lydia. The message continued, "Last evening, Mr. Robert B. Swaine met an untimely death in his office on site in Office Building One. He was apparently struck on the crown of his head by a person or persons unknown.

"The Addison detectives are currently investigating the homicide, and the crime scene has been cordoned off to anyone not involved with the work of the police force.

"We are also mourning another death that took place today at the East Forge Conference Center where the national assemblage of corporate relations communicators is currently holding their yearly meeting. Ms. Christina Benderhoff was murdered in her own room this morning, and we have no information regarding the details of the crime as of yet. The police are just now collecting evidence and interviewing those who were in the vicinity.

"As you can well understand, we are beyond shocked and dismayed over the loss of our colleagues, and until we know more, we have nothing else to report to you at this juncture.

"Unless you have specific business in the corporate relations area of the site or have information pertinent to either crime to relay to the police, please do not attempt to enter the west corridor of the first floor of Office Building One or go to the East Forge Conference Center for more information. There will be none available.

"To talk to the police about anything relevant to this investigation, please contact Detective Joseph Ruschak of the Addison police force. We also ask your patience with the vehicle congestion that currently encompasses our site. Although the traffic is moving very slowly at the entry and exit ramps due to the need for the police to identify each individual entering or leaving the area, please be patient as you will be able to exit within a reasonable amount of time. I thank you for your kindness and cooperation."

Lydia replayed the recording and routinely tidied up her office. It was all she could do to make comfort out of catastrophe. She looked at the phone once more with curiosity. That's so like Karen, she thought. So unruffled. I wish I could get myself together like that, so my nerves and sadness wouldn't be so obvious. But how else could I feel? Christina was brutally murdered and I found her body!

Lydia put on her coat, scarf, and gloves, closed her office door, and walked to the parking lot. It seemed to take an eternity as she slowly snaked down the road to the exit ramp. Exhaustion finally overcame her as she sat in her car waiting to leave.

After a brief conversation with the security guards posted at the exit, she turned with relief into the westward-bound traffic and headed back to the conference center and Dean for the night.

Chapter Thirty-Four

A somber group of communicators gathered around the dinner tables at the East Forge Conference Center on Monday evening at 6:30 p.m. The out-of-state group members gathered around those who had been required to return to the site during the day to learn more about the crimes.

"We don't know much more than you do," said Randy Goddard, who had been holed up in his office most of the afternoon with the incessant phone calls from politicos wanting to know if the murder was tied to any illegalities concerning Clearview products or Superfund sites.

Randy reported to everyone that he was ill prepared to answer any questions, knowing very little more than what the police apparently knew at the moment.

"Those guys in Washington wanted to know if the bills they supported and favored our production would drag them down if word came out that sullied the company's name." Randy slapped his knee and laughed.

"A guy gets killed in an office that's diagonal to mine, and they're worried about their good names. Hell, all I wanted to tell them was that I was worried about my good ass."

No one argued with his comment.

Lydia, who was seated between Randy and Gunnar Williamsen, was ravenous.

"I feel as though I haven't eaten in days," she announced as she dug into her food.

"The deaths certainly haven't blunted your appetite," said Gunnar casually. Lydia said nothing and looked in Dean's direction. Dean was seated across the table from her, between Karen and Dan Macomber. His eyes briefly met hers, and he smiled before he looked down again at his own

Linda Spear

plate of food.

"And how do you think your press conference went today, Lydia?" said Gunnar in a kindly manner.

"I suppose it was much like any other," she replied, "except that two people were killed and I had to report it."

Lydia looked back down to her dinner.

"It's a hard job you have, my dear colleague. Talking to the trash peddlers about such sticky situations is tough trade."

Lydia decided not to look up to give credence to his claim. She knew exactly how to ply her trade, and he didn't need confirmation of what she did so well.

Randy, picking up on the tension, asked her, "Did you hear about the lottery regarding Swaine's leaving here?" he asked gleefully. "I won!"

"I know, Randy. Congratulations on predicting the death of a colleague."

"Oh, I didn't predict his death, Lydia. I just bet on when he would leave. That's entirely different."

Lydia placed her napkin on the table and said to those still seated, "I've had about enough. I have to get some fresh air."

She walked out of the dining room and noticed that Dean began to rise, thought twice about it, and returned to his seat. She sighed in relief as he sat back down. That was more than she wanted to explain to the others at another opportunity.

Following dinner, Macomber stood up from his seat, walked to the podium at the front of the room, and tapped his fork to a water glass. Lydia sat in a comfortable lounge chair to deconstruct the difficult conversation she had with Gunnar. Why does he make me so angry, she wondered as she stuck her head out of the door. When she heard Macomber's voice, she rushed back into the dining room and sat down.

"I want to thank all of you, whether you work here or in other cities, for your infinite patience during this ugly situation and your infinite skill as communicators in assisting the police in their investigation."

He looked around the room and said, "Those of you who continued with the procedural planning session must have been mighty distracted from your mission, but I understand from your group leaders that much was accomplished, despite the interruptions.

"As for those of you who were required to return to the local site to conduct business in respect to the crisis, I want to thank you for your professionalism and your courage. It took a lot of guts to return to the 'scene of the crime,' so to speak, and try to meet your responsibilities. Let me just encourage you to continue to do more of the same with my eternal gratitude.

"Those of you who can complete the last full day of conferences here, please do so. And those of you who must assist the police with their investigation at the site and deal with the external public, I ask your patience and forbearance. I pray this won't go on for too much longer."

Macomber motioned to Ruschak seated behind him at the podium. "You all recognize Detective Joe Ruschak here. He still needs to talk with some of you regarding Mr. Swaine and Christina, so please make yourselves available to him as needed." Without looking in Ruschak's direction, Macomber sat down.

The communicators slowly left the banquet room and filtered in the adjoining studies and libraries that comprised the first floor of the stately manor house. But most of the participants sped downstairs to the cocktail lounge. Detective Ruschak followed them at full speed.

As Lydia left the room for a second time, Dean caught up to her, leaned down, and murmured in her ear. "Meet me in my room at nine," he asked quickly.

Lydia looked at him anxiously and said, "It has to be my room at 9:30. The police may still want to discuss media coverage with me, and I have to be accessible, even by house phone."

"Don't forget to leave the door unlocked," he whispered, and continued to walk past her toward the lounge.

Gunnar sidled up to Lydia again and asked her, "Why was your friend Dean not at the press conference?"

"Why don't you ask him, Gunnar?"

"I just wanted to know how someone who is so involved in your interests wasn't there."

Lydia turned sharply and said, "He apparently couldn't get away from his phone to attend it."

Lydia decided to walk out into the clear and bitterly cold night air. Despite the freezing cold temperature, she sat on the stone retaining wall that surrounded the gardens adjacent to the main building.

Checking her watch, she realized that she could not go back into the buildings because she could easily be caught up in more conversation with the others and miss her time with Dean.

In a stealthy manner, feeling almost shameful, she walked quickly back to Cromwell House and past the room in which Christina died, now cordoned off with the familiar yellow tape that read, "Crime Scene – Do Not Cross." The thoughts of the day made her pick up her pace to reach her room in record time.

Before she entered, Lydia looked mechanically up and down the corridor, seeing no one. With door closed, yet unlocked, she tore off her clothes and rushed into the shower, allowing the hot water to soak her entire body for the third time that day.

Fully relaxed by the hot water, she hardly heard the door open and close. A split second of fear enveloped her. What if the person who entered her room was not Dean?

Without forethought, she pulled the shower curtain across her body and she saw him, half undressed and ready to join her.

They wrapped their arms around each other and let the hot water splash over them.

"I got worried for a moment that it wasn't you when I heard the door close," she said to him after a lengthy kiss.

"Where were you earlier? I kept calling from the cocktail lounge to see if you had gotten back any sooner, but you didn't answer."

"I'll tell you about that later," she murmured in his ear, "but now I just want to enjoy you."

Chapter Thirty-Four

Lying on the bed together, wet towels in heaps on the floor, Lydia molded her body to Dean's. She thought about how wonderfully the scent of soap clung to his skin. Lightly, he brushed his hand up and down her arm.

He laughed and pulled her closer to him.

"Are you completely relaxed, or will it take more effort on my part?"

"It's effort, huh?"

He laughed and pulled her closer to him. "Now tell me, what transpired today when I wasn't around to protect you?"

"Later," she said.

"I've spent my day imagining how you'd look in your underwear, totally undressed, standing up, lying down..."

She interrupted him to say, "Have you had any time to think about other things with all the thinking you've done about me in these various positions?"

"Hardly any," he said in a voice more relaxed with the invitation of her warmth.

She felt their thighs graze each other in an exploratory manner. He lightly touched her neck with his fingers as he lay beside her. Neither one spoke as he drew his hand across her breasts and deftly stroked her torso. She shivered with pleasure and apprehension as his hand explored the rest of her body.

"Dean, you know I've never been a patient woman," she chattered quickly, "and I'm having trouble waiting to feel you inside of me now."

"That's just like you with everything," he replied. "You always say what's on your mind, but just let me show you what else you can have before that."

Dean delicately kissed her erect nipples as he continued to stroke her. He felt her excitement become more urgent.

With aching awareness, Lydia felt her sexuality come alive with more intensity than she could remember. Waves of pleasure arose from her very being, and she undulated to the increasing movement of his mouth as he met the force of her climax with little restraint.

She seemed affixed in a place all her own when Dean pressed his body to hers and entered her. The continuous sensation of her climax was directly evident to him as he matched the pulsation of her body with the strokes that he took within her.

Without awareness, Lydia wrapped both her arms and legs around him and felt none of the weight of his torso as it met hers.

They lost touch of time as they swayed to the rhythm they had established in the union.

As Dean reached climax, he sighed deeply and Lydia cried out in response to his pleasure. The movement of their bodies slowed, and as they lay spent in each other's arms, their senses again slowly reached an awareness of their surroundings.

Lying quietly as time passed in an indeterminate manner, Lydia laughed. "Seems like we should be smoking in this non-smoking room and drinking champagne, don't you think?"

"Yes, and we can order some, if you like. But tell me, what kept you from returning to your room after dinner?" he asked.

Lydia recounted the conversation she had with Gunnar and how she had to hide to escape him.

Dreadful sadness followed, as she remembered her last conversation

Linda Spear

with Christina.

"Do you think that Chris saw more than she was able to remember, Dean?"

Dean propped himself up with the pillows against the headboard, and thought for a moment before he answered. "I think that Christina tended to get bent out of shape for no reason. I'm not discounting that she was outside in the parking lot—that sounds like the truth—but it could be that she imagined some of what she thought she saw while she was out there."

"Dean," Lydia said with some alarm. "She did see someone in white with red splotches on his or her clothing, leaving a car and returning to the hotel. Since we're the only group who is staying here this week, it had to be one of our people."

"Why couldn't it have been someone who went out to a convenience store to buy a box of Twinkees, for God's sake? You'd like that, wouldn't you," he said affectionately as he tickled her belly.

Lydia sat up and said, "But Dean, she was afraid of being accused of somehow being involved in the crime. I can see how she felt. If I didn't remember portions of what I did last evening, and I thought I was in places that I shouldn't have been, I would have been scared too."

"I see your point," Dean conceded.

"That's what I told her," replied Lydia, calmer than before.

"Another thing." She sat up even straighter and crossed her legs, yoga style. "Did you hear Karen's message this afternoon?"

"Yes, what of it? Isn't that what the police told you two to report?"

"Yes, but it just struck me that she was taking the opportunity for self-aggrandizement. You know how she loves to be center stage and be known as the source of all that's holy. I saved the message, I don't know why, but I'll play it for you tomorrow if you want to hear it again."

"It's hardly what I want to hear, Lyd. I hear more of her than I'd like to as it is."

"You know, we haven't even discussed who we think could have committed the crime. I know it wasn't Christina who killed Swaine. I know it wasn't you," she said as he grabbed her and pulled her down, covering her body with his own.

"You were too busy with other responsibilities to have gone to the site to knock off the really big swine."

Dean quickly kissed her, and kissed her again with more intensity. When he moved away, Lydia noticed a sense of sadness on his face.

"What's on your mind?" she asked, aware that his mood had changed.

"I was thinking about having to go back to my house on Wednesday evening and not being able to hold you like this, or talk with you at the spur of the moment, or..." He put his head down before he completed his sentence.

Lydia consciously decided to remain mute. He's a married man, she reminded herself. It's not up to me to decide how he wants to conduct his life. I'm only responsible for my own—I learned that long ago, she recalled. He pressed his face tightly to hers, and she felt tears stream down her face. She knew they were not her own.

Chapter Thirty-Six

Tuesday Morning, January 7

Security was even tighter than the day before at the entrance of Clearview Chemicals, as the employees waited for clearance at the guardhouse. Lydia arrived early to avoid the crush at the site entrance. When she arrived at her office, she cautioned herself regarding her words to Detective Ruschak.

I have to pound this information into that man, Lydia reminded herself. He's got to know how seriously troubled Christina was with what she thought to be an alcohol-induced dream. Since yesterday, however, I'm certain that her so-called dream may have indeed happened and has a connection to the case.

He's going to think I'm a crackpot, Lydia thought to herself. I know it. He may be skeptical as he was before, but when I repeat everything to him with more clarity, I hope he'll take me seriously.

And to support that theory, the maid will no doubt remember that Chris wasn't carrying a handbag when she asked to be let back into her room. As Lydia recalled, that purple dress didn't even have pockets.

"No," said Lydia to herself, more buoyantly. "Now we're getting somewhere. She evidently saw someone out in the parking lot, but she never left the area. That means that she was a witness to something other than the murder itself, but that's how she ultimately became a victim. Who the hell killed her?"

Lydia honked her car horn with the hope of speeding up the procession to the security gate. She had to get to Ruschak. She looked toward the sky and said to her friend, "Chris, I owe this to you.

<u>Chapter Thirty-Seven</u>

Lydia sat at her desk and collected messages as well as any information she needed to pass along to the police and the employees. The file that contained Karen's background and the reason for her behavior lay in front of her on her desk.

Now's the time to ask her, Lydia mumbled to herself as she left her own office, file in hand.

Karen's office, down the corridor from her own, was her destination. She abruptly stopped at the open door and looked inside. Karen was nowhere in sight.

Could she be in someone else's office discussing the issues, or did she not come into the office today in order to further execute her plans for the end of the conference?

Lydia slowly walked back to her office to pick up her phone messages and answer emails. She knew she would rather do this work than deal with the grisly details of the murders.

As she turned on her computer, Detective Ruschak stepped into her office and said, "I'm sorry I didn't get to talk with you again last evening, but you left abruptly and I didn't know in which direction you went."

"I went back to my room at the conference center, Detective. The things that happened yesterday wore me out entirely, and I just went to bed." That was partially right, she thought.

Ruschak casually sat down in the chair across from her desk and pulled out a file folder with a thick stack of papers within.

"I have the ME's report regarding Christina's death," he said. "I thought you'd want to know how it all transpired."

Linda Spear

Lydia sat up straight, pulled her desk drawer open, and grabbed a package of TastyKakes Butterscotch Krimpets. Without pause, she undid the paper wrapper and quickly began to eat her treat as she stared at the detective.

"You do want to know, don't you, Lydia?"

"Of course I do, but I should have offered you some of this before I just ate it all," she said instinctively.

Ruschak laughed and opened the file.

Harold Mendendorf, M.D., M.E.

3702 Gatesby Avenue

Addison, NY 10954

<u>**CONFIDENTIAL**</u>

Date: January 7, 2014

Subject: Christina Benderhoff

Reference Number: 6179195

Name of the applicant for the report:

Detective Joseph Ruschak,

Addison, NY Police Department

Address: 5900 Lincoln Boulevard

Addison, New York 10502

RE: MEDICAL REPORT

1. Patient's Particulars

Name of Patient	Christina Benderhoff
NRIC No.	6939307
Age & Sex	Female—age 36

2. Reason for requesting the medical report

Subject is the alleged victim of homicide. Full autopsy is required to ascertain clinical cause of death.

3. Background information

Christina Benderhoff, female, age 36, and single, was a woman in basic good health who worked at Clearview Chemicals for 11 years. She predeceased her parents who live in Albany, NY. Patient's personal information forwarded from her doctor indicates that she was prone to anxiety and depression, as well as allergies to pollen and mold.

4. Doctor's observations or conclusions

Patient appears to have suffered from acute anxiety and depression for which she was prescribed Zanax for anxiety, Prozac for depression, and Ambien for sleep. At the time of her death, which was approximately targeted at 1:30-2:00 pm on Monday, January 6, 2014, there were strong indications of toxicity from a mixture of alcohol and drugs in her bloodstream and an overdose of the prescribed medications.

Linda Spear

A total of 15 stab wounds were found on the subject's neck, chest, arms, and abdomen, indicating a major struggle and a great deal of rage on the part of the perpetrator.

The victim bled out almost at once as the weapon, a knife with a serrated edge, sliced across major blood vessels in her neck, chest, and major digestive organs.

5. Doctor's opinion on the patient's death

Patient's cause of death was due to the deep stab wounds inflicted to the midsection of her body and her neck. Defense wounds were observed on both her hands and arms. Judging by the severity of the injuries, death was unpreventable by first responders. The spleen was ruptured by the stab wounds, and her lungs were partially shredded, causing a fulmination of blood in the core of her body. Victim bled out as a result of the gouges and puncture wounds. The preliminary toxicology report also indicates a close proximity to coma due to overdose from prescription drugs.

7. Doctor's qualifications

Dr. Mendendorf is a board certified pathologist of 37 years. He is also board certified in internal medicine.

Signature of Doctor
Harold Mendendorf, M.D., M.E.
Name of Doctor
Harold Mendendorf, M.D., M.E.
MCR No. 6470369218
Date of Report: January 7, 2014

Lydia scanned the medical examiner's report as she shook her head back and forth in recognition of the impact of Christina's wounds and the ferocity of the attack. She cringed at the shocking evidence of Christina's heavy drug usage.

"The forensic account of the incident was also included in the file," said Ruschak. "The blood spatter in the bathroom, the walls of the bedroom, and the closet indicated a fierce struggle between the victim and the person responsible for the acts. Even though your friend was considerably weaker than her attacker due to the ingestion of all the drugs, she put up a good fight.

"One point in the autopsy indicated that she was struck on her body by what appeared to be a shoe heel, based on the print. It came down hard on her abdomen, where it penetrated the skin. In fact," Ruschak said with a pained look on his face, "it actually penetrated her liver."

"My poor friend," Lydia mumbled. "That awful group interrogation was the last time I saw her alive."

Ruschak looked sympathetically at Lydia and paused for a moment, then continued. "The thin heel print was decidedly from the shoe of a woman. Now, may I have the file back, Lydia?" Ruschak said quietly.

Ruschak returned to his official posture and said, "Since you are not a member of her family, I am not supposed to share these facts with anyone but the crime investigators and her parents, who have yet to arrive to make arrangements for the body. But I figured that you had to know in order to assist me."

Lydia handed the file back to the detective and sat back in her chair. "I guess there was never anything I could have done for her," she told him. "I thought she might still be alive when I found her, although I could see in her eyes that she was gone. What do you make of the woman's heel print?"

Ruschak changed the subject. "Have members of the media continued to haunt you about the particulars?"

Lydia turned to look at her blinking phone and scanned her list of incoming text messages. She vigorously shook her head up and down.

"I know I have to get back to them today or they will make up their own stories as to what happened to Swaine and Christina."

She looked back up at Ruschak and said, "You never told me the facts about Swaine's death. I only remember that you mentioned to Sergeant Guinness while you were in my office that he was struck twice on his head and nothing more. Could you fill me in on the rest?"

"Not yet, Lydia." Since you were not a party to that death scene, I can't divulge any more to you. Just tell the media that the police investigation is ongoing and we are considering several persons of interest."

"Who?" asked Lydia with a start. "Please tell me who you think may have committed these crimes. Is it the same person for both?"

"I can't give you that information, only that we are deeply involved in ferreting out the criminal party or parties. You know, half of what we do is to eliminate those who have no motive. The other half is to look closely at those who stand out in the crowd. Now I'll take something from your sweets drawer."

Ruschak reached out his hand as Lydia dug into her deep drawer of goodies and gave him her favorite chocolate cupcakes.

"I have to tell you that I admire the work our medical examiners do. It's a lousy job as far as I can see. Everyone who watches *CSI* thinks that being a coroner is glamorous work.

"While that might be true in some circles, for the most part those who work with the coroner's or medical examiner's offices find it a much more mundane and unattractive job. In reality, there aren't any fancy laboratories with huge, clear computer screens lining the walls or all the latest high-tech gadgets to determine if a person's last meal had more starch than protein. Nope. It's a long and tedious day-to-day routine with very few 'aha' moments.

"The coroner's office handles accidental deaths, as well as those of people who die alone or without medical attention. Most of the cases are pretty boring.

"Then there are the homicides like these. And these don't happen as frequently as those television shows would like you to believe. These cases *are* the ugly ones, requiring the coroner's office to send us out to survey the place where the crime occurred and then begin piecing together exactly what happened.

"One time, I was called on to move the remains of a woman who weighed over 450 pounds and lived in a high-rise apartment building. She had been dead for at least a week during a heat wave."

Lydia's face screwed up in disgust as she visualized that scene.

"There were so many flies you couldn't even see your hand in front of your face. And, despite the fact that our officers on the scene opened the windows, the odor of decay was overwhelming. Her body was so swollen that the first time we tried to lift the body, her skin split."

He realized that he was making Lydia feel worse than before and said, "You can just imagine the rest. When people want to know if our job or a medical examiner's job is really like television, this is the story I tell them."

"How can you handle that day after day?" Lydia asked with disgust.

"Fortunately, it's not day to day. Not even week to week," he said with relief on his face. "The reality is that most of us wade through death scenes, stepping around blood and body fluids, trying not to gag over the smell. All the while, we do our best to make an accurate determination of what happened. Picking up pieces left from a dead body after trauma is not at all like you envision. It's somewhat like defining a type of road kill.

"And as I've mentioned, sometimes it's hard to tell that the pieces you're picking up were once human. But fortunately, I only see this type of death now and then. It's a once in a while gruesome event, but we never forget or lose the respect for what or who was once a human being."

Lydia looked the detective in the eye and said, "How long does it take until you get those images out of your mind?"

He rose from his chair and replied, "Never," as he waved goodbye to her and nodded in thanks for the treat.

Ruschak rounded the corner outside her office as Lydia let down her guard and clenched her teeth in anger over what the detective told her concerning Christina's hideous death. The image of road kill stuck in her mind.

Chapter Thirty-Eight

After Detective Ruschak left, Lydia decided to wash her face. Although she wore little makeup, her face was no doubt streaked with mascara that had run down her cheeks. Tears had become a constant occurrence for her within the last twenty-four hours.

As she dashed into the ladies room, she noticed that Karen was combing her hair at one of the mirrors. A spray here, a spray there, and it was perfect as always.

"Hi Karen," said Lydia with as little enthusiasm as she could muster.

"Hello Lydia," she said warmly. "Are the media hounds making your life holy hell?"

"Somewhat, Karen. You could say that I make it easier on myself by speaking to them through email and text. That, in itself, takes up a lot of time and self-control, but it's easier than the non-stop phone calls. One thing is for sure: It's not a great time to be a public relations manager in charge of output to the information hustlers."

Karen smiled, pursed her lips together to be sure her lipstick was even, and patted Lydia on the back.

"It will all pass, Lydia. You'll see. I'm just doing my job as best I can too and waiting for the police to wrap this up and get the hell out of our lives."

At that very moment, Lydia remembered the file on her desk pertaining to Karen's former job at Andrus Chemicals.

"Karen," Lydia said quickly, "I have something to show you when we get back to our offices, so please hang around so I can come in and discuss it with you."

"Sure. I'll be in for the rest of the afternoon. Bring in a couple mugs of tea if you remember so we can relax for a while and have a nice chat," Karen said sweetly and moved toward the door with a broad grin on her face. She turned to face Lydia again and asked, "By the way, what do you think of the conference?"

"Well, to be perfectly honest," admitted Lydia, "I haven't had much time to participate in it. You know I had to hand over my presentation to Mary Zappia from the Anaheim group to deliver since I couldn't be there. I hope she did a great job. All she had to do was read what I wrote and let the slideshow do the rest."

Karen nodded and said, "Yes, it went very well. I helped Mary arrange that, and I gave the handouts to Dan, which he delivered to the rest of the group when she finished her presentation.

"Sorry you couldn't have gotten the praise you personally deserved for what you wrote and planned to say," she said. "It was wonderful and completely in line with the way you are handling this issue."

With that compliment, so rare from Karen, she turned and walked out the ladies room door.

Chapter Thirty-Nine

As Lydia, walked back to her office, face freshly washed and dried, she noticed that Karen was sitting erect at her desk, evidently immersed in her work.

Lydia sighed and looked at the file folder staring her in the face from the middle of her desk as she arrived back at her own office. It hadn't been moved since the day before, but she knew it contained damaging information that Karen would not expect her to know and would not be willing to discuss.

But first, she knew she had to return calls or email the members of the media to update them on the investigation.

Hours later, several reporters offered to take her to dinner in exchange for additional information. Some even alluded to more indulgences for all the information gathered thus far. Lydia politely declined each offer and contemplated about how long this travesty would continue.

She picked up the phone to call her sister, Emily.

The phone rang only once when Lydia heard Emi's cheerful voice on the other end of the line.

"I heard about what happened at your company," Emily yelled into the phone. "I prayed that none of it involved you."

"Oh, Emi, I'm so glad to hear your voice. It's been a madhouse around here, and I can't wait to get away from the lunacy that has taken over this place. Can you imagine that every day, until the case is solved, I have to talk to the press about two murdered souls? One of them was my friend."

There was silence at the other end of the line before Emi spoke.

"Why don't you just leave now and come home? I'll be at your place as soon as I can make it. We had plans to get together soon anyway, so let's make it this weekend."

"That sounds good to me, Emi, but it will have to wait till the weekend. I hope you don't mind doing absolutely nothing but eat takeout food, sleep, and watch TV. But it will be a great relief to me."

"Perfect. I'll be there with your TastyKakes supply and some other goodies. If you can get a couple dozen fresh bagels—all kinds please—that we can freeze over the weekend, I'd be very happy."

"Of course I will," Lydia replied, "and I'll have the smoked salmon and cream cheese ready to go with it. I can't wait to see you."

"Me too, sugar. Just get through this hideous business and we'll relax in the comfort of your own home and avoid the crime shows. Okay?"

"Deal. Love you, Emi, and thanks."

"Love you too, sweetheart."

With the last email, text, and phone conversation completed, Lydia happily put the phone back on the receiver and turned to Karen's Human Resources file.

Without forethought, she took the pages from the folder, made copies of them all, and placed the originals in her desk with the drawer locked.

Although she had no tea to offer, just the file, Lydia walked down the hall to Karen's office. Karen barely looked up as Lydia entered.

"Have a seat, Lydia. I'll be with you in a minute." Karen continued to make notes on her calendar, paused for a moment, cocked her head, and decided to put the work aside. Smiling cordially, she asked, "No tea? Hmm... What's on your mind, Lydia?"

Lydia thrust the Human Resources file in Karen's direction. Unsure of what Lydia held in her hand, Karen at first shrunk back from Lydia's assertive movements. Lydia placed the file on Karen's desk and stood silently as Karen tentatively picked it up.

The woman blanched as she quickly leafed through the file and snapped it shut. "Where did you get this?" she hissed.

"It was sent to Swaine's office yesterday morning from Human Resources, and Angela, who is handling his mail, gave it to me. What does it mean, Karen?"

"Why do you, of all people, need an explanation?" Karen countered, clearly angry at the intrusion.

"Your name, it's not Karen Paulson. It's Anne Diamond. Why did you change your name?"

Karen's eyes darted back and forth, looking beyond Lydia at the doorway.

"Lots of people change their names," she said defensively. "In my case, I decided to go back to my maiden name. I thought you knew that I was married once, but I had no children so there seemed to be no reason to hold onto a name I no longer cared to use.

"As for the name, Karen, it's actually my middle name, and I always liked it better than Anne anyway. Satisfied?" She said to Lydia with contempt, holding fast to the file.

"No. That's the least of it. What I really want to know is why, if you already knew Swaine from your time at Andrus Chemicals, you kept that fact a secret when he came on board. And why didn't he indicate that he knew you already?"

Karen paused, deep in thought. "I don't know why the hell I'm letting you grill me like this, but I would guess you'll go directly to your buddy Detective Ruschak with the file if I don't give you everything you want to know, so I'll tell you."

Karen stiffened in her seat and put the file in the top drawer of her desk.

"I actually decided to change my name around the time I left Andrus. I also decided to let my hair grow and highlight it. I also had some cosmetic surgery for the parts of my face that didn't please me."

She carefully touched the ends of her hair and leaned back shaking it out. "I always wanted to be a blond, you know, and figured that if I had gone so far as to change my name, I might as well change my looks too."

"And Swaine?" Lydia probed further.

Karen sighed. As her shoulders fell forward and hunched toward her desk, she swung her body to face Lydia and leaned back against her chair again.

"The truth is that Swaine simply didn't recognize me. There was no point to telling him who I was. He was a major reason for my departure from Andrus in the first place."

"How so?" said Lydia, more sympathetic.

"He was there to do essentially the same thing to that company that he was hired to do here. You know that anywhere he goes he uses his hatchet on the staff. I got caught in the crossfire. To draw attention to the fact that he could do that to me again would have been foolish, I'm sure you'd agree."

It all made sense.

"All right, Karen," replied Lydia, apologetically. "I'm really sorry I bothered you, but I still have to give the file to Detective Ruschak. After all, it was sent to Swaine. Anything that Swaine was concerned with on the day he was murdered has got to be included in the investigation. You understand, don't you?"

Lydia reached out to receive the file. Karen stood up and firmly blocked the drawer of the desk where she had placed it.

Lydia moved closer to the desk with her hand out. "Karen, I need the file back. Please give it to me."

In a plea for compassion, Karen said in a small voice so as not to be heard by others, "Lydia, don't you understand? If the police get hold of this information, they are sure to reach the wrong conclusion about me and Swaine, and even Christina, and they will assume I committed the murders."

Shaking her head, Lydia countered, "Why would you have anything to do with Chris' murder? If you're not guilty, Karen, you have nothing to worry about. You can certainly explain what you already told me to the police."

Unmoving, Karen shook her head and then said shrilly, "You don't know anything about that beast, Swaine." Her face swiftly contorted to that of an enraged animal.

"He made sick moves on me, Lydia—absolutely disgusting. Do you know what it's like to have a creature like that unzip his fly, expose himself, and tell you how you can earn your paycheck and benefits?"

Lydia saw the tortured look in Karen's eyes and backed up, anxious to leave. "I'm sorry that you've been through something as awful as that, and I truly sympathize with you, Karen, but I don't intend to be pulled into a cover-up. I'm going to have to tell the police about the file. You can tell them the rest."

As she turned and walked toward the doorway, Lydia felt a searing stab of pain in her shoulder blade.

"Holier than thou bitch!" Karen shrieked. Stunned, Lydia turned to see the enraged woman, arm raised with a letter opener in hand and about to strike again.

"Stop, Karen, stop!" Lydia cried out as she tried to reach the door. She felt her shoulder being twisted from its socket as the desperate woman grabbed Lydia's arm and viciously wrenched her backward with the letter opener poised at her chest.

Karen, with a firm grip on Lydia's arm, restrained her from leaving the office and stabbed at her chest and neck several times with all her strength.

Lydia's frame involuntarily convulsed at the incessant spikes of pain from the torturous pulling force on her shoulder and arm.

With a sudden burst of energy, Lydia jerked free of Karen's grasp, and with her arm hanging limply at her side, she ran wildly toward the door. Karen stopped for a split second, and made one final effort to stop Lydia with a stab in the middle of her back.

Panic gathered in Karen's eyes as she pushed past her injured colleague and made it to the door. She then turned in the opposite direction of the gathering crowd in the hall and took off toward the nearby stairwell.

Ruschak heard the commotion and peered out from Swaine's office. There he saw Lydia, blouse ripped, holding her left arm against her body, stumbling toward him.

Before he could utter a word, Lydia yelled, "It's Karen. She's the one! She tried to kill me."

Ruschak dodged passed her, yelling, "Secure the perimeter!" He was followed by one of the nearby police officers, who took off in pursuit. Sergeant Guinness, with calm assurance, placed a call to security to apprehend Karen at the parking lot entry. "Restrain the woman, Karen Paulson, once you spot her," he yelled to the patrolmen behind him.

Trembling and crying in pain, Lydia limped toward Dean and

faltered as she sank to the carpet.

Dean was wholly mystified as he stared at her in shock. He reached out to wrap his arms around her, but she involuntarily screamed when he touched her lifeless arm.

"My God, Lydia. Oh my God."

Macomber, Goddard, Williamsen, and the others stood in their doorways, alternately gazing down the hallway and back to the badly injured woman and the man who tried to comfort her.

Dean gently lowered Lydia to the carpet and took off his suit jacket to cover her wounds and torso.

Guinness stepped out of Swaine's office holding his cell phone. "Security spotted Karen as soon as she left the building and nabbed her at once," he said, well satisfied with his own efforts on behalf of the capture. "Get an ambulance over here to Office Building One, first floor, STAT," he yelled into the phone.

Guinness then spoke with Ruschak and learned that, although Lydia put up resistance, Karen had been arrested and read her Miranda rights.

"He said he'll be taking her down to headquarters for questioning, and he asked me to look after you, miss. How can I help you?" Dean brushed Guinness away and tenderly touched Lydia's ragged blouse. He carefully tried to connect the torn shreds of fabric that exposed her injured torso and shoulder.

Lydia slowly pulled away from Dean and looked down at herself in horror. Her sleeve had been wrenched away, and rivulets of blood appeared to be dripping from her body, arms, and hands for the second time in two days. Her left arm hung uselessly at her side.

Dean carefully reached for her blouse at the shoulder and gently pulled it aside, revealing several deep stab wounds inflicted by Karen's letter opener.

"Lydia, what happened?" Macomber asked repeatedly.

"I wouldn't even know where to start."

Grimacing in pain and trembling uncontrollably, Lydia listened for the rescue sirens. In less than four minutes, an ambulance arrived. With Dean's help, the emergency medical technicians moved Lydia's injured body to the gurney, and within seconds they were on route to the nearby medical center.

Chapter Forty

At the Addison Medical Center, Lydia was whisked into the emergency room, where she was examined by Dr. Edwin Turner, the emergency room physician on duty, and several nurses who had been alerted to her tenuous state before arrival.

After Lydia was hooked up to intravenous fluids, an IV antibiotic, and an oxygen mask that covered her nose and mouth, a blood panel was ordered and drawn for testing. Lydia's wounds were counted, examined, and compressed to stop the bleeding. The dislocated shoulder, which caused her the most pain, was put back in place.

After the shoulder was reset, Lydia could not stop sobbing.

"She wanted to kill me," she continued to moan. "That horrible woman wanted me dead like Christina. She stabbed me with all her strength. I was sure I was done for. I could have ended up just like Christina." She cried all the more. "Poor me. Poor Christina."

After the full examination was complete, Lydia's wounds were cleaned, dressed, and sewn shut.

"She's lucky that these wounds were inflicted by a dull-edged letter opener instead of a sharp-edged weapon," explained Dr. Turner. "She did, however, lose a lot of blood. Her major organs, determined by an MRI, have not been touched, but her shoulder may need surgery down the road. We will be able to determine that in about a week or two when the swelling comes down and she comes back to get the stitches removed. We will also judge the progress of the shoulder reset. She's a very fortunate woman to be alive."

"Yea. Lucky me," Lydia mumbled sarcastically, remaining barely awake after having received a morphine injection for the pain.

Linda Spear

"Did they catch Karen?" she asked the attending nurse who monitored her vital signs.

"I don't know, dearie," the nurse answered kindly. "You'll have to ask the police about that. Your vital signs are stable now, you'd want to know, and it appears as if you will be fine.

"Just be careful. Do not move that arm. Your shoulder is in a very delicate state. You must keep the bandages and the sling close to your body."

Lydia breathed a sigh of relief. The morphine had kicked in, and except for a bit of blurred vision and pressure on her arm and shoulder, she no longer felt the acute effects of the attack.

"Nurse, would you call Detective Ruschak over here so I can find out if that monster is still on the loose?"

"Of course I can," she answered in a composed manner.

How can she be so calm, thought Lydia, when I was nearly hacked to death?

"But I have to see her," she heard Dean yell at the same nurse who tried to explain that Lydia needed rest.

"Hell with that," he replied more calmly. "She's hurt and I should be with her."

A sea of uniformed medical professionals followed him into Lydia's cubicle. There he saw Lydia, heavily bandaged, left arm in a sling, and eyes half closed. Despite it all, she had a broad smile on her face.

"Oh, thank God you're alive," he said as he tried to kiss her. She flinched.

"Oops," he said sheepishly. "I didn't think that a kiss would cause you pain."

"Only when you kiss me leaning on my semi-detached arm," she replied. "But I'll be alright," Lydia said slowly. "I heard the wounds were not as deep as they thought, and the shoulder needs rest, but I'll heal up fast, you'll see."

"I just want to take you in my arms and make the whole thing go away," he said in misery. "If only I could have been in there to protect you. I didn't have a clue that you were in so much danger. Detective Ruschak told me the whole story while we waited to see you," he told her.

"What did he say?" asked Lydia, more alert than before. "I told him some of what happened in Karen's office and more when I first got here. Then they started working on me and pushed him out of the way. I need to see him to tell him the rest. Can you get him over here, Dean?"

"I'll look for him. He's back from the stationhouse after dealing with Karen's arrest. He and I had a long conversation while we waited to see you, so I'll fill you in on everything later. But tell me," he asked, "Why were you in Karen's office?"

Lydia slowly told him how Angela had come across the file meant for Swaine and had given it to her. When she read it, she realized that Karen and Swaine had worked together at Andrus Chemicals when Karen had been let go.

From there, she told him about Karen's change of names and appearance before she joined Clearview.

"No one knew of her former association with that man. I feel so stupid for running into her office and showing her the proof of her treachery," Lydia said mournfully. "I really just should have shown it to Ruschak while he was in my office and let him deal with that crazy bitch."

"We always think of what we should have done after we have done it," Dean replied soothingly. "I'm just so grateful that we were all there when it happened and that they got you to the hospital before you lost more blood."

Linda Spear

"Will I be able to leave here tonight, Dean? Do you think they will let me out of here? Please make it happen, please." Lydia pleaded and continued to ramble as Dean caught a glimpse of Ruschak coming toward them with a huge grin on his face.

Ruschak reached out to grasp Lydia's hand, and his touch was met with yet another wince of pain.

"Everything hurts, Detective, but I think my toes can handle a foot shake."

Dean and Ruschak laughed to hear that Lydia's humor had not been wounded.

"The docs say it's a miracle that none of your major organs were affected," he sighed with relief. "They say you may be released a little later this evening, after they continue to follow your breathing patterns."

Lydia looked at Dean and mouthed "thank you" to him. He looked down at her bandaged body with sadness and nodded.

"But what about Christina's murder? Is Karen responsible for that too?"

Ruschak's grin escaped the planes of his face. He nodded abruptly and asked, "Are you up for the whole story?"

"Whoa!" Lydia tried to sit up to hear the rest but collapsed back on the hospital bed.

"You relax, young lady. I'll do the talking, and you just listen."

Ruschak pulled up a chair and went into the lengthy explanation of what happened at the conference after lunch on the first full day.

"She committed the murder, of that we're certain. It seems that Karen heard Christina talking about seeing the purported clown in the parking lot, and she realized that Chris had seen her return from the corporate site with blood all over her white dress and coat.

"During the group interview, she took a steak knife from the table—you know, the one she used to peel her orange at lunch—and placed it in her purse knowing she had to get rid of Chris before the police could hear everything and put together the meaning of what she actually saw. The fact that she used a knife on her victim showed a huge amount of forethought and a definite level of intent.

"Chris knew that she had said too much at that interrogation in front of the group, one of whom she believed could be the murderer. That's when she ran to her room to pack and leave—fast. Karen followed her back and accosted her in the bathroom. She first plunged the knife into Chris' body as she trapped her in the small room, as she had her cornered by the sink.

"Chris fell to the floor and attempted to crawl away from her attacker, but she only made it as far as the closet, where she tried to protect herself by attempting to close the door.

"But Karen was relentless. She held the door open with her foot and continued to plunge the knife into Christina while the dying woman lay helpless. That's referred to as overkill."

Ruschak took a deep breath and continued.

"But this is the most incredible part of all, Lydia. Karen was covered with blood again and knew she could not get back to her room in that condition, so she grabbed a dress of Christina's and changed into it, balled up her own ruined outfit, and casually walked back to her room, which was just a few doors away."

Lydia, for once in her life, had nothing to say. Her mouth hung open, and Dean took the opportunity to pinch it closed. She smiled slightly as she grasped the dark humor in the whole episode.

"Guinness went to her room after the arrest and found the bloodied clothing, which included Christina's purple dress gathered up with Karen's outfit in a plastic laundry bag.

"Everything has been sent to forensics and will be shared with the medical examiner today, as he is currently finalizing Swaine's autopsy and will have all the findings available to us by tomorrow."

Dean reached out to shake the detective's hand. "You settled this case in record time for us to be together to hear the news. Thanks so much for your dedication to this case, Detective. It is so awful to know that we lost Chris to this killer, but you never left the area and you stuck with the sources who gave you the most information. I cannot tell you enough how I admire your skill."

Lydia looked askance as Dean expressed his unusual effusive behavior, then she asked, "When we return to the conference center, Detective, are we allowed to discuss this with our colleagues?"

"To the extent that they were involved, you can. I know you are anxious to put this to rest," he replied, "but I advise you to let me tell your colleagues the entire story. Over time what we are ready to release will come out. You know that the information regarding these murders has not yet have come to light for the general public. I haven't even taken your formal statement yet. We can do that later when you are feeling better.

"But don't talk about the information you got about Karen's stint at Andrus Chemicals, Lydia. We don't want the public to start questioning people at that corporation about her behavior there.

"Warn the others to keep what they know to themselves. And you, young lady, just take the time to get well and let us handle the police procedures. I'll see you later so you can give me your statement."

Dr. Turner pulled back the curtains of the cubicle where Lydia rested, poked his head in, and said, "I'd like to admit you for an overnight to be perfectly sure that you have no more bleeding episodes or too much pain to handle."

"Then I'll sign myself out," Lydia insisted. "I don't need anything more than your prescriptions to get through this with Dean."

Dr. Turner turned to Dean, whose worried face showed that he needed more input from the doctor.

"Doctor, please give me a printout of what I should do to help her when we leave. I'm kind of skittish because I've never taken care of anyone with serious injuries before."

Dr. Turner shook his head and said, "That's why I'd like to keep her here, Mr. Handlesman. The best you can do is guess if something happens to her that you cannot handle. Do you realize that you have a considerable amount of responsibility for a badly injured woman? She may be in a great deal of pain that requires more than the medication I can prescribe in pill form, and there is always danger of a serious infection that flares overnight. That's something that only we can treat with IV antibiotics. If she leaves in your care, it falls to you to act on her needs, you know."

Dean nodded and took Lydia's hand. "We'll get through this together," he said as he looked directly at Lydia's determined face.

"Alright," replied Dr. Turner, and he shook his head in resignation while he signed the discharge papers. "I still want to keep an eye on you for an hour or two to be perfectly sure. Your nurse will give you the discharge papers at that time. Good luck, Ms. Barrett," he called out. "If you run into any problems at all with swelling, additional redness around the wounds, bleeding, or trouble breathing, please come back in immediately—and I mean pronto. Some of your injuries are tricky and may need more attention. Even a plastic surgeon may need to look at them at some point."

Lydia smiled, and as she weakly shook the doctor's hand, she winced with the slight pressure. "Thanks Dr. Turner. I think you were the second person to save my life today."

<u>Chapter Forty One</u>

Tuesday, January 7, 7:00 p.m.

The mood in the main dining room at the East Forge Conference Center was decidedly more relaxed than the night before. The contingent of communicators who had remained at the center and continued with the task at hand appeared to be well satisfied with the results of their two and a half days of intensive work.

As they mixed their conversation with bits of information discussed in the meetings with the outcome of the police investigation into Swaine's and Christina's deaths, curious eyes followed Dean as he carefully helped a heavily bandaged Lydia to her seat at the table. She sat in a portable wheelchair loaned to her by the conference center.

Lydia, for her part, was oblivious to the commentary yet grateful for the support that surrounded her. Despite the prescribed antibiotics and pain-killing narcotics, her wrenched arm, torn from its socket by Karen and firmly put back in place, was now cushioned and supported by a heavy duty sling.

The bandages that covered the puncture wounds on her torso rubbed uncomfortably against her loose-fitting sweater. The waistline of her pants had to be left unclasped so as not to dislodge the lower wound coverings.

"Does it hurt?" asked Dean.

"If you mean my whole body, yes," Lydia flippantly replied.

"But is it worse," Dean countered. "I want to be able to call Dr. Turner and tell him if things have changed."

Those who watched the couple from a distance could easily detect the intimacy that had changed their relationship within the past few days, and Macomber, who stood drink in hand with the group from Boston, watched with concern. The grapevine among the group was rife with gossip.

"We heard the whole story from Ruschak when he returned from police headquarters," said Dean. "He wanted to know whether Lydia was going to be released from the hospital, and I cannot tell you how happy I am that she's here with us."

Dean carefully retold the others of the frightening events that took place at the site. He recapped what Detective Ruschak had deemed appropriate to divulge.

"It comes down to the fact that Karen had previous dealings with Swaine at the company where she worked before. I can't divulge what company as it could bring them bad press if the name leaks out. Their press relations should not be connected to ours.

"But it seems that she was accused of stealing pharmaceutical formulas and selling them to a competitor. Anyone with any sense would know she wouldn't have access to this information, but the fact remains that whether or not she could be guilty of this, Swaine and two other members of senior management accused her of grand larceny.

"But because they obviously could not supply the burden of proof, they gave her the option to immediately resign and take nothing with her but their recommendations. With those testimonials, which were quite complimentary, and none of the accusations to follow her, she was easily able to land a job with Clearview," Dean continued.

"Although Karen looked familiar to him, he didn't recognize her when he first appeared on the scene at Clearview because of the name change and her dramatically altered appearance. She also kept a low profile in the few days at work prior to the conference, as much of her time was spent organizing the conference at the center, away from the office.

"The recognition actually came to him when they were face to face at the first dinner, as she stood to be acknowledged for her work and he walked in on the announcements.

"She became frighteningly aware of the distinct look of recognition, and she knew that she had to justify her performance and ask him to keep her past quiet.

"Instead of going straight to her room at the end of the night, Karen left through the back exit and arrived at the corporate site by 10:30 p.m. Security at the entries and exits had been disconnected all through the day and night because the air vents were being checked in the 'sick buildings.' The workmen were in and out of the buildings, and no one expected an intruder to be on the grounds at that time.

"She worked her way undetected into our corridor and apparently confronted Swaine, who was sitting at his desk, about the evidence he had threatened to reveal that exposed her as a corporate security risk to Clearview.

"He probably laughed out loud and asked what she'd do for him to ensure confidentiality. I bet she innocently said that she would undertake any program he had in mind for simplifying his operation.

"This afternoon, while she was being arrested, she told Detective Ruschak that Swaine said she could renew their relationship with oral sex. So he unzipped his fly and reached for her. That's when the quick-thinking Karen grabbed his heavy, oversized beer stein and smashed the top of his forehead in an attempt to stop him. That's why he flopped forward on his desk.

"She no doubt panicked and made a quick search of his desk drawers for evidence of any references he had gathered on her and found none. Actually, we found out a while ago that it was sitting on Ms. Ashworth's desk all the while, until Angela took the mail to sort the next morning.

"Karen was smart enough to leave his overhead light on, even after having to defend herself from the man, but she closed his door and left through an open side exit.

"She returned to the conference complex around 11:30 p.m., when we know that Christina went outside during the night for some air to walk off the booze. That's when she saw Karen enter the complex in her white wool dress and coat and covered in blood. Since Chris was outside by herself and anxious not to have her boss see her in a less than desirable state, she said nothing then, or the next day. And Karen, in her haste to get back inside, did not stick around to notice anyone that she heard.

"Meanwhile, back at the ranch," Dean interjected in his monologue, "Frenkle and Ferguson saw that Swaine's light remained on, and they noticed his form hunched over the desk through the beveled glass. So they decided to leave the guy alone, not wanting to start an argument as to why they were there. Then they completed their check, still without finding the source of toxic leakage into the system.

"The next morning as the day progressed, Miriam got increasingly uneasy. That's when Miriam checked on him and found him dead. And for all her trouble, she suffered a heart attack from the unbearable stress.

"So Angela was the real hero in the situation," interjected Randy.

"Yes, that's for certain," replied Dean. "Angela heard Miriam call out for help, and she quickly called for the emergency team on site to administer first aid. They immediately called 911 for an ambulance to take Miriam to the hospital.

"And you know the rest. The police arrived at Clearview to deal with the site of the crime, and Ruschak came to the conference center to question the members of our department. And that's all, folks!"

"But what about Karen?" asked Randy.

"Well, Detective Ruschak said she's in a holding cell for now, waiting to be arraigned for the attack on Lydia. But the truth of what

Swaine had said to her, and how she responded in self-defense, all came out this afternoon when she was arrested.

"During her interrogation, she admitted to the police interrogators that she killed Christina as well because she recalled hearing someone in the parking lot when she returned to the site with blood all over her clothing. She realized later that it was Christina.

"Karen also told the police that Swaine had sexually harassed her on a continual basis while she was at her last job, and when she rebuffed him, she firmly believed that he retaliated by cooking up the formula theft story."

"Well, why didn't she just deal with it openly?" asked Renee. "It was really dumb of her not to reveal what was perpetrated against her."

"It wasn't that simple," answered Dean. "She told the police that she didn't think anyone would believe her, and when, in her anger, she started to envision him dead, she got scared. It wasn't arrogance that steered her in that direction. It was fear and rage. She was so totally disillusioned by Swaine's ugly betrayal and ouster that she decided to change her whole persona before seeking a new job. She let her brown hair grow long and dyed it the blond color it is now. Then came the cosmetic surgery. She told the police that she even changed her type of makeup and the way she dressed. She just wanted to make a fresh start."

Grudgingly Renee replied, "Well, I guess I can understand that."

Dean continued. "As you well know, everything went well for her until Swaine made his entrance at Clearview. Karen was worried sick from the moment she laid eyes on him, and she feared that he'd instantly recognize her and start to terrorize her all over again, even after her whole reconstruction.

Lydia's mouth was agape. "Can you imagine the kind of fear she had that she might be savaged all over again by that guy?"

Dean shook his head in amazement and continued to reveal all of the information he had learned from the detective.

Detective Ruschack also told me that Karen said that after she hit him, blood had spattered all over her coat and dress, but she checked for vital signs.

"When she reached for his wrist and drew his arm toward her in search of a pulse, she said his body twitched convulsively. She told the police that she felt as though her heart would stop because she sincerely believed he was still alive and was reaching out to grab her.

"So that's where she left him, thinking he was still alive," said Dean as he sighed with the weight of the entire story.

"She dropped the beer stein on the carpet, slammed the office door, leaving the light on in his office, and apparently left the same way she came in, unnoticed by Frenkle and Ferguson, who were on the premises but must not have been nearby at the time.

"Karen was aware of someone else's presence in the parking lot back at the conference center. When she returned to her room, she thought that she might not have gotten back without being noticed. That began to worry her all the more.

"After hearing her story," Dean added, "the police said that when they searched her room this afternoon, they found the bloodied white dress, coat, and gloves in one of the plastic laundry bags. They also found Chris' purple dress among her own clothing. Lucky for us, she apparently hadn't had the time to dispose of any of the evidence."

Dean continued to tell everyone how Lydia had received the Human Resources file from Angela, apparently ordered by Swaine before Karen showed up at the site that night.

"Swaine probably left a message to send for Karen's file on Miriam Ashworth's voicemail when he arrived at the site on Sunday night.

She must have gotten the message when she came to work first thing on Monday morning.

"After she called Human Resources to order Karen's file, she no doubt erased the message from her machine. That's why the file arrived first thing on Tuesday morning in the interoffice mail, addressed to Swaine. Fortunately, it was found by Angela, who was handling Swaine's mail and showed it to Lydia."

"What in the file made you suspicious?" Renee asked Lydia.

Lydia shook her head in disgust. "It revealed that she had previously worked with Swaine and that she had been known as Anne Diamond, not Karen Paulson, while she was employed there. That, in itself, made me suspicious, so I went into her office to talk with her about it.

"What tipped me off, though, was that she tried to kill me. Fancy that. I always believe that's always a good indicator of an existing problem," she said with a sigh. "And you know the rest."

With mouths gaping wide, the group of friends did not know whether to laugh or cry.

Dean ran the back of his hand gently down her cheek. "I'm glad she didn't slice up your sense of humor," he said. The group continued to watch with sordid interest as their colleagues appeared wholly different in their relationship than they had before.

The din of silver tapping on crystal drew everyone's attention to the head table, where Macomber stood once again. He handed a sheaf of papers to the waiters with instructions to hand one out to everyone assembled.

"Ladies and gentlemen," he said with a serious demeanor. "I've spoken with various members of the media in regard to today's situation, and I gave them the press release that is being handed to you at this time. As you know, Lydia Barrett is currently unable to continue in her role as the corporate spokesperson at this time due to the injuries she sustained earlier today.

"If there is anyone who is unfamiliar with what happened at the site and the current status of the Swaine homicide, additional information will be forthcoming to all employees throughout the corporation tomorrow.

"I want to announce that Miriam Ashworth is making steady progress toward recovery, and her doctors have moved her out of intensive care. She's been placed in a semi-private room. Visitors, I've been informed, are still being kept to her immediate family. I'm sure, however, that she'd appreciate a card or two from her friends."

Macomber continued. "This conference, I'm sorry to say, has been dwarfed by these tragic events: the murder of a member of senior management and a friend and colleague, as well as the arrest of an employee who, I have been informed, will enter a plea of diminished capacity at her arraignment. Because of legalities, I can say no more to you on these subjects at this time."

There was silence in the banquet room as everyone stopped eating and paid rapt attention to the speaker. Pointing in the direction of Ruschak, Macomber added, "I want to add my sincere appreciation to Detective Joseph Ruschak and his team of investigators.

"They conducted a thorough and responsible investigation, and we as a unit are grateful that the cooperation of our employees aided in their resolution of the crimes in such short order." Heads turned in Lydia and Dean's direction, and they looked quickly at each other. Dean smiled broadly and Lydia lowered her eyes.

"Tomorrow, we will have our wrap-up meeting, and Charles Wainwright plans to address the group." Macomber deftly avoided mention of the fact that Swaine had originally been scheduled to speak at that time.

"So relax tonight, everyone. Drinks in the cocktail lounge are courtesy of Clearview Chemicals!"

<u>Chapter Forty-Two</u>

Seated at a small table in the corner of the dark, oak-paneled cocktail lounge following dinner, Lydia was sitting with Dean. Renee Trottier and the other communicators from Shreveport made note of the fact that Dean and Lydia were oblivious to the voices of the people around them.

Some of the others looked uncomfortable as Lydia referred to her foray with Karen, just hours before. Dean abruptly stood and excused himself to make a phone call.

As he walked away, a roar of laughter arose from a table nearby. "Sweet Jesus," exclaimed Randy Goddard. "I can't believe it! That son of a bitch Swaine brought me good luck!"

A chorus of "What happened?" came from a table across the room.

"I won the lottery on when Swaine would be leaving the company! Lucky for me," he added gleefully, "we didn't have to pick the way in which he would leave us. Everyone said I was a stupid ass to choose a time only hours away. It was wishful thinking on my part, I suppose, but hell, I won twenty-two hundred bucks!"

Lydia felt her wounds begin to throb and rose from the table, telling the group that she was going to rest. "I left my medication back in my room, and I need to take it now."

Randy noticed the discomfort on Lydia's face and asked, "Do you need help getting back to your room?"

Lydia, expecting to see Dean said, "No thanks, Randy. I'm doing fine. Go back to the party, and don't worry. All I need to do is rest, but thanks again."

Lydia slid into her wheelchair and slowly moved up the handicapped ramp next to the stairs. Toward the main entrance to the Converse House she met Dean on his way back to the lounge.

"Where are you going?" he asked her, anxiously taking hold of the wheelchair.

"I need to rest," she said, now visibly trembling with exhaustion. "I think the entire thing finally got to me."

Dean turned back in the direction of the exit and collected her overcoat from the check room, placing his own gloves in her coat pockets in case she needed them later. He carefully helped her to stand as he secured the buttons of the garment over her body so that she was fully covered.

With one arm wrapped protectively around Lydia, they went back to Cromwell House. No longer concerned about being observed, he took Lydia's key and opened her door, following her wheelchair inside.

Slowly, he sat her to the edge of the bed and helped her out of her clothing, first removing the sling that held the dislocated shoulder in place and then inching the sweater off her body.

She cried out in pain as Dean helped her remove the rest of her clothing and eased her onto the bed so that she could sit. Only when he needed to get a glass of water for her to take her pain medication did he relinquish his support. He then returned to her side and slowly replaced the sling.

"You've been wonderful," she said. "In truth, I don't think I could have managed this alone tonight." Dean remained quiet as he lifted her legs so she could slide under the covers. Lydia rested her shoulders against the propped pillows and looked at Dean with love and gratitude.

"Christina would have been glad to help you if I wasn't here," he said simply. He did not meet her gaze as he spoke.

"Who did you call before?" she asked him with sudden apprehension.

As she made herself comfortable under the covers, he turned and began to remove his own clothing.

"Tell me," she repeated.

"She's pregnant."

"Who's pregnant?" Lydia asked, not fully comprehending.

"Patti. I spoke to her on the phone a little while ago. She went to the doctor today to verify a home pregnancy test she took yesterday. The doctor says she's five weeks pregnant."

Dean, his back to Lydia, repeated the words without emotion. For several minutes, neither spoke. As if on cue, they began to speak at the same time.

"You first," he said.

"I think you should go back to your own room tonight, Dean." She slowly inched further under the blankets to fully cover her nakedness. "It must be very painful for you to be with me." Lydia's voice, he noticed, had become a monotone.

He turned and sat next to her on the bed, grasping for her uninjured hand. "I didn't want to hurt you this way. You've got to believe me, Lyd, but I have to figure out what to do." His voice cracked as the words poured forth.

"When you were getting your wounds treated in the hospital today, Guinness asked me, point blank, what was going on between us. He is, after all, Patti's cousin, and I wasn't ready for that."

"So what did you tell him?"

"I told him..." He paused. "I had to lie. I told him we were just close friends. I know he didn't believe me."

She gently removed her hand from his, and avoiding his glance, attempted to turn her body to the side. But as she maneuvered, her face contorted in pain and he reached out to help her.

"Please leave me alone, Dean. I need to be by myself now." Desperately, she wanted to cry, to scream, to release the physical and emotional pain, alone.

"I can't leave you in this condition, Lydia. I need to be with you tonight. It may be selfish of me, but I do, and you know you need me too."

She inched away from him. "Do what you want," she said, in an attempt to sound indifferent. "But would you please turn off the light? I need to sleep."

Without hesitation, Dean turned off the light on her side of the bed and walked to the other side, stretching his body alongside hers. He turned on his side to face her and gently placed his arm around her waist.

Lying stone still, Lydia hoped the darkness would prevent him from seeing the devastation in her eyes. Dean could not draw away, and he wrapped himself around her body for what he knew might be the final time. Despite her efforts, she could sense that Dean had abandoned stoicism, as well. All that was left was an aura of lust and sorrow.

Chapter Forty-Three

Wednesday, January 8, 8:30 a.m.

Placed on every seat in the large conference room of the East Forge Conference Center were neatly typed updates on the criminal investigation. With Joe Ruschak's input, Macomber had prepared a statement to employees regarding the recent events at the site. Together, they had delivered the completed transcript to corporate headquarters to be sent to all the sites via email.

Lydia very slowly and carefully walked into the banquet room, unassisted, after asking a bellman to go to her room to take her luggage to the lobby. To occupy herself, she picked up a copy of the update and began to read what had hastily been prepared the night before.

DATE: Wednesday, January 8

SUBJECT: Homicide Investigation Update

Clearview Chemicals

Addison, New York Site

On Tuesday, January 7, the Addison Police Department apprehended a suspect in the murder of Robert B. Swaine, Vice President, Administration, and Christina Benderhoff, Communications Specialist, Internal Communications. The homicides, which took place on Sunday evening on site at the Clearview Chemicals corporate headquarters and Monday afternoon at the East Forge Conference Center were singular events in the history of the company.

The alleged perpetrator, Karen Paulson, Manager of Internal Communications and an employee of Clearview Chemicals for over four years, entered a plea of diminished capacity at her arraignment.

Ms. Paulson, currently being held in police custody without bail, has enlisted the support of the law firm of Downey, Burkhardt and Rice. Douglas Burkhardt, a defense attorney who specializes in criminal litigation, will be assisted by members of the Clearview Chemicals legal team, as needed.

Any additional information pertaining to the case should be brought directly to the attention of Detective Joseph Ruschak of the Addison Police.

Clearview Chemicals strongly discourages employees from talking directly to the media regarding Ms. Paulson, Ms. Benderhoff, or Mr. Swaine.

Lydia felt the presence of eyes looking over her shoulder. "I think your team deserves a lot of credit for getting this out to everyone so quickly and doing it in spite of the day you had yesterday," said Renee.

Lydia nodded to her friend with gratitude.

"Where's Dean? I felt sure that he'd be with you this morning," said Renee. "Otherwise, I would have come over to help you dress and get your luggage ready to take home. I didn't want to intrude," she added with a wink and a smile.

Lydia replied quickly, "Don't worry. He helped me, but he just hasn't come down to the banquet room yet."

Renee searched Lydia's face for a sign. She saw none. "What's going on between you two? Everyone's asked me. You didn't make a secret of it last evening, you know."

Lydia's face contorted. "Whatever it was, Renee, it's over. I was totally delusional about the relationship. That's nothing new for me." Lydia paused, swallowed hard, collected her thoughts, and volunteered, "He did help me dress this morning, but then he returned to his own room to pack up. There's nothing more to say."

Lydia smiled weakly and added, "My sister, you know, the one who lives in Philadelphia? She's on her way to my condo now. I called her and filled her in last evening before dinner. She loves to be a mother hen. She'll stay with me through the next week and longer if I need her. You'll appreciate this one. She told me she's bringing a huge stash of TastyKakes!" Lydia forced herself to smile, although her eyes were brimming with tears.

"I'll be fine. Trust me on this one. I'll be fine!"

Renee took a long, hard look at Lydia, and uncertain of what she could do, said, "Well, if you're sure that you're alright, I have to get on with the stuff that Karen was supposed to do for the final session." Renee began to walk away, but looked back at her friend with fondness and said, "I'm going to keep my eye on you, anyway, even from a distance. You're a good friend, Lydia. Don't forget to stay in touch for any reason."

Exhausted from a sleepless night, Lydia sank into a nearby chair, waiting to gather some additional strength before attempting to get a cup of coffee and some pastries from the buffet table.

She thought about the last of the Butterscotch Krimpets that remained in her suitcase and wished she had the good sense to put the package in her purse before leaving her room, but at that point, when Dean left her side, she didn't feel at all hungry.

She recalled the time she spent with him that morning. They had spoken little. He sensed her needs as she moved stiffly about the room, and he chose clothing from her suitcase for her to wear, placing it gently on the bed after he helped her bathe.

Her arm, she noticed, felt tighter, more painful than the day before. The shock had worn off and the second part of the healing process, which she had been told about when her shoulder was being reset in its socket, had begun.

The shoulder had throbbed as Dean re-bandaged the puncture wounds on her upper back and torso.

"I think you should see your own doctor when you get home," he cautioned her, almost as if to make neutral conversation. Lydia remained silent.

Fully dressed with Dean's help, packed and ready to leave, Lydia stood by the door, staring at her lover. Dean had not yet finished dressing and stood in his undershirt and slacks, shoeless.

In as matter-of-fact a manner as she could muster, she said, "I'm leaving my suitcase in the room. I arranged for a bellman to put it in my car before I leave." Dean nodded silently, watching her with trepidation.

"You look so lost," she said to him, revealing her pain. "No, it's really me who feels so lost," and she began to cry. Dean reached for her, arms extended, but she turned her head aside and put her free arm up, palm facing his direction. He stopped and waited.

She turned to him again. Protective anger was all she had left.

"I'll say this once, Dean, and you'll never hear it from me again. I love you, and that's more painful than anything I feel from my shoulder and these stab wounds."

She looked down at her helpless arm and said, "You know, I've probably loved you from the first time I met you. But up until this week, I had the good sense not to admit it to myself. What a fool I was to allow this to happen."

Dean's mouth dropped open and he sighed heavily. Tears flowed from his eyes. Lydia opened the hotel room door and looked back once before she left to see his head buried in his hands.

Chapter Forty-Four

Renee Trottier pulled Lydia away from her thoughts. "I came back to see if you had eaten anything yet," said Renee, followed in tow by three members of the Shreveport group.

Lydia shook her head from side to side, and Renee offered to bring her breakfast back to the chair where Lydia rested. As Renee turned toward the buffet table, Lydia noticed Dean enter the conference room. He appeared to scan the crowd, and his gaze stopped when he spotted Lydia seated in the back row of the area cordoned off for the conference itself. He began to walk toward her and watched her painfully struggle to her feet. She purposefully started to follow Renee, who insistently took hold of her uninjured arm and gently returned her to her seat before returning to the buffet table to collect coffee and food.

At that moment, Randy Goddard joined Dean, slapped him on the back, and said, "So, how do you think I ought to spend my lottery money, Dean old buddy? On a vacation, a down payment on a new car..."

"Save it," said Dean abruptly and walked away.

Randy looked curiously after Dean, who continued to watch Lydia, surrounded by the others.

Tapping on the microphone and clearing his throat, Dan Macomber spoke clearly. "Will everyone pleased be seated? We are ready to begin the final session of the Communicator's Conference."

As everyone slowly wandered to their own spot, he began.

"Thank you for your prompt attention this morning. With a little luck, we can complete this meeting before noon and give those of you who are traveling a good distance some time to get to the airport so you can spend some time at home before you go back to your desks tomorrow.

"As you can see," he said carefully, "some changes have been made to the agenda, due to the recent events that have overshadowed the original plan for the conference, of course.

"First on tap will be the people designated by each of the three focus groups to report their findings, followed by a response and closing remarks from our Chief Executive Officer, Charles Wainwright.

Macomber introduced the first speaker and returned to his seat.

Within an hour and a half, all three speakers who represented the work groups had laid out their individual market strategies, and following a lengthy round of applause for the speakers, Wainwright moved to the podium to speak.

Lifting the microphone away from the stand, Wainwright stood next to the podium, leaning his elbow on the flat surface, hand to chin.

"As some of you know, each time I come to the East Forge Conference Center, I make sure to save some time to swim in the beautiful indoor infinity pool. In fact, I've swum a few laps with some of you."

Wainwright waited to see if his comments had eased the tension that permeated the room. Seeing no change in his audience, he continued.

"This week, recreation of any sort wasn't in the cards. Yet, it seems strange that so much could happen in three and a half days. It also gave me pause for reflection.

"Although I had not planned to speak at this conference, as you know, I'm glad that I now have the chance to address some problems that I should have dealt with some time ago.

"Beyond all the disturbing events that have taken place over the past few days, I'd like to tell you about some of the positive things that have happened. It's become painfully clear to me as I listen to you today that communications between various layers of the organization have not been forthright, and that's my responsibility. I plan to pay more attention to that.

"You'll also be pleased to know that over the past weekend, Paul Frenkle and Cal Ferguson conducted an indoor air quality inspection in Office Building Two. This course of action needed to be done over the weekend when the building was not open for business.

"After an exhaustive investigation, in which the two men reviewed the occupants' activities and the building functions, it was determined that all heating, cooling, and venting systems were in compliance with state regulations regarding volatile organic compounds. Odors emanating from unsealed ducts revealed several raccoon nests and the remains of partially decomposed rodent bodies.

"Progress is already underway to clean, disinfect, and deodorize the affected ducts, as well as make the minor alterations with sealant that are necessary in the ductwork, air diffusers, and return air grills. I am grateful to these men for undertaking the scope of this repair and restoration.

"I am alarmed, however, about the breach in security that may have contributed to the death of Robert Swaine on site," he added. "But actions have been taken to see that safety measures will be put in place so our well-being will not be violated again." Wainwright paused and there was a smattering of applause.

Renee leaned across Lydia and said, "I wonder how he punished Frenkle and Ferguson for leaving the door open. He'll probably make them hang out together after work for a month with no brewskies." Lydia laughed. It felt so good to enjoy even a moment of relaxation. Renee's probably right, she thought, as she recalled the obvious animosity between the two.

"Now on to a more difficult topic," Wainwright said, almost apologetically. "These are tough times in which we live and work. The economic downtrend has required that all businesses take a hard look at department functions and the resultant expenses in order to cut back on duplicated or unneeded services.

"This fact of life is, unfortunately, something I had to consider as the head of Clearview Chemicals.

"My decision to hire Robert Swaine, who was well known within the industry as a brilliant strategic planner and organizer, was based on the assumption that he could objectively define the necessary roles within each corporate department and increase the cost effectiveness of every function. I have since reconsidered that my idea to facilitate this process may have been faulty."

Wainwright paused again to get a sense of his audience, who remained unmoved. He resumed his speech.

"According to the police, who have kept me informed on their careful investigation of the crime scene and thereafter, Mr. Swaine, I'm told, may have had some personality characteristics that led to his unfortunate demise. As time goes on, we will no doubt learn more about the incident itself, the victim, and the person accused of both of the crimes, and we will be able to draw more educated conclusions.

"It is unfortunate that this ugly chapter in our company's history has become so public and has hurt so many. But, judging from the presentations that I heard today, you, as our company's communicators, were able to get on with the task at hand and plan the role of communications and marketing for this and future years to come. You obviously have a concrete grasp of what it will take to promote the inherent value of Clearview Chemicals well into the twenty-first century. I thank you for that.

"I also thank Daniel Macomber for keeping a cool head during this tough time, and hope that he will remain with Clearview for many years to come. I've personally asked him to continue to steer his department as he has so ably done for so long.

"Now before it gets too late and I become the one who makes our travelers late for their planes, let me wish you all well as we look forward to this new year with hope and optimism. Thank you."

As Wainwright began to step away from the podium, he heard one set of hands clapping and looked up to see a broadly grinning Macomber on his feet, followed by the rest of the crowd who joined him in a growing thunder of applause. Obviously grateful for the show of support, Wainwright gave the "thumbs up" sign.

Macomber called out, "Don't ever do that in Australia, Charlie. They take that to mean that you're flipping the bird!" Wainwright, laughing, lowered his hand and walked through the room, shaking hands with those on the aisles as he passed.

Macomber walked to the podium and took the microphone. Lydia noticed that for the first time since before Christmas vacation, Macomber did not have a straw clenched between his teeth. "Thanks for everything, people. You did an incredible job, each of you in your own right. Get home safe!"

Lydia gently hugged various members of the crowd, saying goodbye. A sudden burst of pain radiated from Lydia's shoulder as she felt Gunnar Williamsen bump into her chest and injured arm. As she winced in pain, he looked at Lydia with contempt.

"How is our little superwoman this morning?" he asked with considerable sarcasm.

Lydia, about to respond with anger, decided to say nothing. But Gunnar did not retreat.

"What happened to your playmate, Handlesman? You two have a little lover's spat?"

"Gunnar, drop it, will you?" she said without emotion. "I can smell the alcohol on your breath," and she looked away.

"You weren't in your shower last Sunday night when I knocked on your door, were you, Lydia?" Gunnar stood back, arms folded, a sneer on his face.

Lydia shook her head in disgust and turned around, but Gunnar stepped in front of her.

"I saw you go into Handlesman's room around nine. In fact, I thought you saw me because my watch beeped and you looked around for the sound. Aren't you glad that I didn't mention that fact to your pal the detective when they were still investigating the murder?"

"Gunnar, you are slime," Lydia hissed as she attempted to push by him. He held his ground by fixing his hand on her uninjured shoulder. Lydia was temporarily trapped. She thought quickly and decided to take a long shot. She motioned for him with her index finger for him to come closer. His head faced hers, inches apart.

"I know about your affair with Karen. I know all about it. Do you want me to mention to Ruschak that you may have been an accomplice to the murder?"

Gunnar gasped, releasing his grasp of Lydia's shoulder. "How did you know? You couldn't have known. You were too wrapped up in your own dirty little fling." He shook his head with scorn, took one step backward, turned, and made a quick getaway.

Chapter Forty-Five

As Lydia slowly made her way to the door of the conference center lobby, she saw Dean waiting in front of the heavy oak entry doors. For a moment, she considered turning around and waiting in a nearby conference room until he left, but considering that Gunnar was probably still close by, she moved ahead toward her luggage, which waited for her near the door.

Dean walked to meet her, and taking her able arm, led her to the side of the lobby where few people gathered. She turned away from his gaze.

"I'll leave her," he said suddenly, his voice husky. "I swear it."

"You'll do nothing of the sort," Lydia snapped with annoyance. "Do you think that I would even consider being with a man who could walk away from a pregnant wife?" She shook her head to emphasize her point.

"But I love you, Lydia, I really do. We'll talk about this again—at the office, tomorrow," he said, looking into her face optimistically.

Lydia forced herself to remain impassive and formally replied, "I won't be back at the office until I'm feeling well enough to work. In any case, we won't discuss this ever again. I mean it, Dean. We'll talk about business at the office when necessary and nothing more."

She walked slowly through the parking lot to her car with a bellman following closely behind her. Stabs of pain infused her shoulder, chest, back, and sides as she forced herself to rest a minute and lean on the side of her car. She popped the trunk so that the suitcase and her briefcase could be placed inside. Lydia made an effort to tip the man, but he refused her offer and she thanked him profusely as he bowed slightly and left.

Her thoughts fell to Angela, who was working so hard at the site but without guidance. She hadn't even called to ask for help.

With one hand on her cell phone, Lydia punched in the numbers for 1-800-FLOWERS. Within a few short minutes she had ordered a dozen red roses for her assistant to be sent to headquarters with a card that read, "You are my hero. Love, Lydia."

Renewed strength filled her body as she climbed into the driver's side of her car, turned the key, and became thankful that her injured arm was not the one needed to get her car in gear.

She felt the buttons of her coat strain from the bulging objects within her coat pockets. Then she remembered what was within.

With her left hand, she removed the gloves left there by Dean when he helped her into the coat and buttoned her securely before they returned to her hotel room the night before. She felt the lush suede fabric and remembered the feel of his skin. She smelled the leather and felt a lump in her throat.

Overwrought, she reached across herself and pulled the other glove from the left pocket. She threw them both angrily to the passenger seat of the car and began to drive.

When she reached the exit point, she looked back to see Dean leave the lobby and walk toward a red Mini Cooper. Should I give him the gloves? Her mind raced to make a decision. A young blond woman left the driver's side of the car and walked around to greet him, extending both arms. The woman, no doubt his wife, was pretty, very petite, and adoring. She looked down and happily patted her still flat belly as he opened the trunk of the car and placed his baggage inside.

His wife slid into the passenger seat as Dean walked around to the driver's side. Dean scanned the roadway, but before pulling away from the curb, he noticed Lydia's car drive toward him. As their eyes met, she strained to open the window and let the gloves fall.

Lydia looked through her rearview mirror and watched Dean drive by the place where the soft, suede gloves rested on the road. She could also see his wife inch closer to him and place her head on his shoulder.

<u>Epilogue</u>

The annual Clearview Chemicals Fourth of July picnic was held without fail at a nearby nature preserve for employees and their families.

The employees who planned the event could count on the number of picnic goers to hover around 1500. The faces, however, changed from year to year. Older children of employees nearing middle age and beyond usually chose to avoid the challenge of making small talk with their parents, the boss, or the boring coworker. The threat of hearing, "Look how big you've grown," or "My, my, haven't we filled out," became much more than many teens could bear.

The ranks, instead, refilled with the newer family additions; babies born during the year, fast-growing toddlers, and preteens whose movements their parents could still control.

Single members of the employee population frequently brought friends to the picnic, but a large number, of which Lydia was a part, considered the employee picnic to be work, plain and simple, to which they chose not to subject those for whom they cared.

One of the topics most discussed at the event this year was Christina's murder and the sad situation of Karen Paulson. Employees recalled how active Karen had been in organizing the picnics of the past and how unlikely and how unfair they thought it was that she was now serving two concurrent twenty-five-years-to-life sentences for the charges of second degree murder of Swaine and Christina.

Gathered around one large picnic table toward the end of the day sat Lydia, legs crossing the bench, sharing a package of Hostess Twinkies with Detective Joe Ruschak, who rolled a volleyball back and forth to Randy Goddard and his wife, Anne.

Angela and her boyfriend, Diego, who was a chef at a major restaurant in New York City, laughed quietly at the way the amateur cooks handled the barbeque.

Paul Frenkle had joined the group for a short while to catch up on the latest news while his wife Susan talked incessantly to all the women present. "I have to hear from you what goes on around this place because all Paul wants to talk about is baseball," she said with reluctance. "I'm sure you know more about what he does at work than I do."

Frenkle looked askance as his wife babbled on and on. After what must have felt like hours, he looked at her and sourly said, "Can't you just shut up?"

Gunnar Williamsen, dressed in crisp white cotton pants and shirt, contemplated the slowly melting ice that remained in his paper cup and swirled it languidly as he watched the impending sunset.

Macomber, who licked the last of the sweet, sticky barbecue sauce from his fingers, casually watched his wife Fiona as she busied herself by packing the remains of their picnic lunch in the ice cooler.

Although a number of plastic straws were still on the table, Macomber managed to avoid placing even one in his mouth throughout the long day. It was an exercise of pride and triumph for the department head, and he silently congratulated himself for having kicked not one, but two oral fixations in little more than six months.

Cal Ferguson was not wearing his hard hat as he walked the park area, making sure that any fires in the barbeque section were well under control. His wife, Samantha, had left him months before because of escalating OCD issues that dominated his presence at home.

As Lydia and Joe Ruschak thumb wrestled on the wooden table, it was Ruschak who caught the first glimpse of Dean Handlesman and Patti as they walked in their direction. Randy gently poked Lydia in the ribs with his elbow. As he continued to eat the ribs, Lydia looked up, pulling her hand away from Ruschak. She quickly straightened her legs, lowering them to the ground and remembering to tug at her rumpled clothing.

Dean approached the table with obvious reluctance. He had spent the large part of the day with employees from the Washington D.C. satellite office, and had managed to avoid the strain of sitting for long periods of time with people who knew more about him than his own wife.

The group was impossible to avoid however, as their table was in the direct path to the nearby parking lot. Lydia impulsively thrust a cupcake in the couple's direction, trying to mask her discomfort with artificial cordiality.

"Twinkie, Dean?" she casually remarked.

Decidedly shaken, Dean gently shoved his very pregnant wife in front of him. With his hands on her shoulders, he said, "Patti, meet Lydia Barrett, Detective Joe Ruschak, Gunnar Williamsen, Anne and Randy Goddard, Daniel Macomber and Fiona."

Patti, small, blond and cherubic, face flushed with the effort of dealing with a summer pregnancy, leaned down to shake hands with each person at the table. Her hand trembled imperceptibly in Lydia's grasp.

Lydia noted that despite the warmth of the day, Patti's grasp had the cold clamminess one associates with either illness or discomfort.

"When's the baby due, Patti?" Lydia asked with feigned interest and a large measure of controlled nonchalance that obscured the soaring tension she felt inside.

"In a little more than four weeks," the pregnant woman responded with obvious pleasure. "I'm kind of nervous though, this being our first baby." She leaned back to catch a look at Dean's face, which had turned to watch the volleyball game being played less than a hundred feet away.

"Well, I'm sure I'll hear all of the fundamental details from everyone," Lydia said sweetly, without changing the tone of her voice. "Good luck!"

Dean, in wide-eyed shock, turned back to face Lydia.

"Didn't you know?" replied Lydia, indifferently. "I've accepted a job back in a tiny suburb of Albany called Hanover. It's a textile manufacturing operation, and I'll be their Director of Corporate Communications.

"I sold my condo, lock, stock, and all the furnishings last Saturday, and I'm out of here in a couple of weeks for a long, deserved vacation in Barcelona. I've always wanted to go to Spain, especially since I learned decent conversational Spanish from Angela and Diego. Then I'll move into my new condo and start all over. The new job begins right after Labor Day. I guess that suits you too, Patti—Labor Day?"

Awkwardly, Dean reached for Patti's hand and began to pull her closer to the bench. She stumbled and fell against him as he hauled her sideways. Lydia leaned forward and asked, "Do you know if it's a boy or a girl?" Patti held out both hands and shrugged.

"Well, if it's a girl, you might want to name her Lydia. I feel as though I've known that little dumpling since she was nothing more than a sparkle in her Daddy's eye."

Macomber shifted uncomfortably in place and reached for a straw. The others pretended not to hear Lydia's words or see their boss' reaction. Lydia cast her eyes downward, somewhat ashamed of her sarcasm yet aware that the others at the picnic table carefully observed her response.

Over the past six months, not one of her colleagues had inquired about the aftermath of her brief, yet blatant, affair with Dean Handlesman, and she recalled the awkward period of time when returning to work made everyone feel ill at ease.

Dean interjected nervously, "Patti, you remember my telling you that Lydia was the woman responsible for exposing Karen as Swaine's murderer."

"Go figure that one out," added Randy. "She was sure a strange one, but not the type I'd picture as a murderer."

Lydia shrugged her shoulders and said offhandedly, "You never know about any individual. I've given up trying to second-guess anyone's behavior."

"And how are you feeling now, Lydia? Are you all healed from the stabbing?" said Patti with obvious concern.

"The physical wounds were quick to heal," responded Lydia in a detached manner, "but the emotional ones are still a little raw."

Dean Handlesman looked flushed, as if he was also feeling the effects of the heat.

"And I certainly don't get any great satisfaction in contributing to Karen's pain," added Lydia, defensively. "It's no secret that she and I were not the best of friends in the office, but the poor woman obviously got caught up in something she couldn't imagine handling in any other way. It's obvious to anyone who knows Karen that she didn't go there expressly to kill Swaine or Christina. I knew her well enough to believe that she was appalled that she was responsible for anyone's death, especially Christina's."

"Still, I wouldn't call bashing in a man's head a socially acceptable means of handling a crisis," said Randy Goddard sarcastically. "Or stabbing her coworker to death. After all, she sought them out, she confronted them, and she whacked him with a beer mug and Christina with a steak knife. Guilty as charged," he said with a chuckle. Goddard laughed alone.

Gunnar Williamsen smirked, glanced at the assembled group, and said in a high-pitched imitation of a woman's voice, "She was so horrified that she whacked him once and said, 'Oh no, that's not enough,' and whacked him again with his own beer mug to finish the job. Sure. She was so aghast that she had to hit him twice," he repeated with sarcastic chuckle.

Though the temperature was in the upper eighties, Ruschak felt a sudden chill and the unmistakable flow of adrenaline to his gut. His gaze, which had been mindlessly fixed on the volleyball, slowly shifted across the table to Lydia's face. Their eyes met, and Ruschak knew instantly that she understood the words to which he had viscerally responded.

No further communication was necessary. Both Lydia and Ruschak turned to face Gunnar Williamsen. His clenched jaw and his closed eyes evidenced his understanding of his fatal mistake. The fact that Swaine had been struck twice had never been made public. There was no way that Gunnar Williamsen could have known that fact, unless...

Ruschak walked directly up to the stricken man and said, "I want you to accompany me to police headquarters to discuss what you just mentioned."

Gunnar looked at the police detective in shock.

"Why do I have to do that?" he asked in a defensive manner.

Ruschak replied, "Gunnar Williamsen, you are under arrest. You have the right to remain silent. Anything you say will be used against you..."

Lydia stood and watched the display in amazement. Could he have struck Swaine with the second blow that apparently was the fatal one? Was Karen correct when she said that Swaine was still alive when she left him? Was Gunnar right on her tracks at the corporate headquarters that night as well, and why?

Ruschak pulled out his handcuffs and roughly placed them on a stunned Williamsen. He turned the suspect around to prevent the man from running.

"He was going to have me fired," Williamsen stammered. "I had to kill the bastard. He was already almost gone anyway when I got to his office. Karen had already taken a swat at him before me. I just finished him off. After all, I am the brother-in-law of the CEO who was going to threw me to the wolves, damn that son of a bitch. How dare he do that to me?"

Williamsen struggled against the restraints and bent his head forward, trying to break way but to no avail. Ruschak steadied Williamsen with a steel grip while turning Gunnar around to prevent the man from running.

As Williamsen staggered towards Ruschak's police car, Dean and his wife moved away from the scene and toward the parking lot. Patti was clearly oblivious to it all. She tugged on Dean's arm and said, "What was that all about?"

Dean shrugged and said, "Nothing that concerns you."

Patti continued to press her husband for facts. "Why won't you tell me what just happened here?"

"Because it doesn't have anything to do with you," he replied in an irritated tone of voice.

But Patti continued to chatter on and on until her husband dropped her hand and started to walk faster. She stumbled along, caught up, and whispered, "When you mentioned Lydia at home, you never told me that she was so pretty."

Patti struggled to catch up with her husband and shouted, "Don't you dare treat me like a simpleton. This subject is not closed. We'll discuss it further at home."

Dean directed his gaze toward the skyline ahead. He noticed the panorama of changing colors in the sunset and sunrise that had once brought him serenity with Lydia, then said in a monotone, "I never gave the way she looks much thought."

The End

Linda Spear